"AND SO WE LEAVE.

As legend has it that men of old first left their place of birth. To venture into the empty dark with nothing but hope as their guide. Shall we find El Dorado? Jackpot? Bonanza? A new Eden? Worlds of mystery and untold wealth lying like jewels among the stars, lost planets or worlds that are nothing more than the figment of dreams. Is that what you seek?

"On such a trip as this who knows what might befall? Life? Death? Riches or poverty, space holds them all. Those who search must surely find. Happiness. Contentment. Paradise itself, perhaps.

"And, who knows, perhaps even Earth itself!"

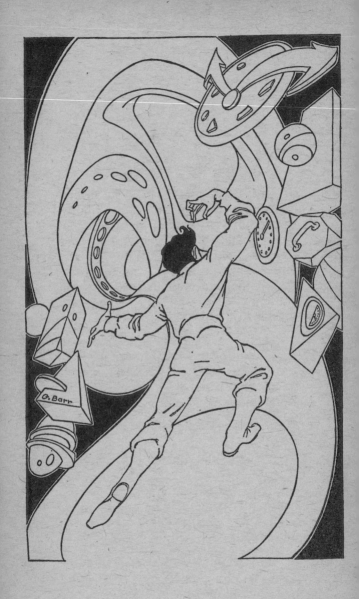

◆ ◆ ◆

Eloise

◆ ◆ ◆

E. C. TUBB

DAW BOOKS, INC.

DONALD A. WOLLHEIM, PUBLISHER

1301 Avenue of the Americas
New York, N. Y.   10019

Cover art by George Barr.

DEDICATION:

To Steven Barham

DUMAREST NOVELS
Available from DAW Books:

9:	MAYENNE	(UQ1054—95¢)
10:	JONDELLE	(UQ1075—95¢)
11:	ZENYA	(UQ1126—95¢)
12:	ELOISE	(UY1162—$1.25)

FIRST PRINTING: MARCH 1975

1 2 3 4 5 6 7 8 9

Eloise

A "Dumarest" Novel

Chapter One

~~~~~~

There was nothing soft about the office. It was a vast chamber designed on functional lines, bleak in its Spartan simplicity; the sound-proofing which covered the walls, floor and roof a dull, neutral grey, devoid of distracting color or decoration. Only the blazing simulacrum which hung suspended in the air at the center of the room gave a richness to the place; a depiction of the galaxy at which Master Nequal, Cyber Prime, stared with thoughtful interest.

It was a masterpiece of electronic ingenuity; tiny motes of light held in a mesh of invisible forces, the entire lens constrained within three hundred cubic feet of space. With such compression, detail had to be lost; the billions of individual worlds, the comets, asteroidal matter, satellites, minor regions of dust, all swallowed in the glowing depiction of countless stars. Nequal touched a control and red flecks appeared in scattered profusion, irregularly spaced but extending throughout most of the area. Each fleck represented a cyber, a trained and dedicated servant of the Cyclan of which Nequal was now the accepted head.

An ancient emperor would have felt gratification at the extent of his rule, but Nequal could feel no such emotion. And there was no need of personal ambition. To be Cyber Prime was to be at the very apex of his world. Even to be a part of the Cyclan was to be a part of a near-invisible empire which would, in time, dominate every known fragment of space.

Softly he walked beside the simulacrum, concentrating; noting gaps, the proximity of concentrations, the blank regions in which no red glimmers showed, turning as the door opened to admit his aide.

"What is it?"

Cyber Yandron bowed. "Those for processing, Master. They await your attention in the reception chamber."

"A moment." Nequal continued his examination, then again touched the control. The projection faded to dissolve in splintered shards of luminescence; the brilliant glow replaced by a more subdued illumination, a blue-white actinic light which gave maximum visibility, rich in ultraviolet for reasons of hygiene. "I am ready."

Outside the office the passages were a hive of controlled activity. Cybers, alike in their scarlet robes, moved soundlessly about their tasks. The air was chill and Nequal almost decided to raise his cowl. He resisted the temptation. The body was a weak and irritating thing; to pander to it was foolish for it grew on what it was fed. And yet the air did strike chill. Perhaps he should order the diet increased a little. Every machine needed fuel, and energy lost in combating cold was energy lost to the efficient working of the brain. He would have the dieticians look into the matter.

A decision made in the time it had taken to walk three paces, another made in the time it took to walk seven.

"Action to be taken on report 237582EM," he said to Yandron. "Have the laboratories concentrate on a cheap and simple method of manufacturing churgol by synthesis from easily available products. The resultant information to be disseminated on the worlds of Sargolle, Semipolis and Sojol."

Churgol was the major export of Churan, a proud and independent world; the others, the main customers for the medicinal compound. Once their major source of income had vanished, the Ghuranese would be less independent and not as proud. They would be eager to seek helpful advice in order to restore their fortunes and be willing to pay for the guidance of a cyber. The thin end of the wedge which would place yet another world under Cyclan domination.

A decision made, a problem solved—he wished that all were as simple.

A small group waited in the reception chamber; the scarlet of their robes warming the bleakness, the material rustling a little as they moved aside to allow the Cyber Prime a clear passage to where five men rose painfully from a bench.

"Be seated." Nequal stepped towards them, his thin

hand extended in greeting. Two were old, two diseased, their bodies bloated in grotesque proportions; the other twitched with an uncontrollable affliction of the nerves. Nequal studied him for a moment, but the eyes were clear and the man would never have been passed by the physicians had his mind been affected. "You, all of you, are welcome."

They bowed where they sat, brief inclinations of their heads, then straightened as they looked at the tall figure of their master. He was old, for men do not achieve great power without waiting, and lean, for a thin body was more efficient than one soft with killing tissue. His face was set in a mask of impassivity; the head hairless, skull-like, the contours relieved only by the glowing intelligence of his deep-set eyes. On his breast, as on the breasts of them all, the great seal of the Cyclan glowed with reflected light. Like them all, he had long ago accepted the truth of the creed which dominated their lives.

The body was nothing but a receptacle for intelligence. Emotion was to be decried, eliminated by training and surgery; the severance of certain nerves leading to the thalmus when young, the operation which left every cyber the living equivalent of a machine, able to find pleasure only in mental achievement. But none counted it as a loss. Only the mind counted, the sharpening of the intelligence, the cultivation of the pure light of reason and inexorable logic.

Traits which made every cyber able to take a handful of facts and build from them the most probable sequence of events. To extrapolate the result of every action and course of conduct. To make predictions so accurate that, at times, it seemed they could actually read the future. A service for which rulers and worlds were willing to pay far more than they guessed.

"You have worked well," said Nequal in his trained modulation. A voice carefully devoid of all irritating factors. "Your dedication, skill and application have earned you the highest reward it is possible for any of us to know. I shall not keep you from it." He gestured at the attendants. "Go now. Almost I envy you."

But there was no need for envy, even if he could have felt the emotion. He, all of them, every cyber who reached old age or imminent death, all who had proved themselves; all would take the same path as the attendants now prepared for the five.

First they would be shown the great halls, the endless passages and vaulted chambers gouged from the living rock far beneath the planetary surface; the entire complex buttressed and reinforced to withstand even the fury of thermonuclear attack. They would see the serried rows of vats, the laboratories, the hydroponic farms; the whole tremendous installation which was the headquarters of the Cyclan.

And then, assured, their gestalt firmed, they would become a part of it.

They would be taken and drugged. Trepans would bite into their skulls and expose the living brains. Attachments would keep them alive, as they were lifted from their natural housings and placed into containers of nutrient fluids. Other attachments would ensure that life continued and that the intelligences would remain awake and ever aware. And then, finally, the living, thinking brains would be incorporated into the gigantic organic computer which was Central Intelligence.

To live forever. To share in the complete domination of the universe. To solve all the mysteries of creation.

The aim and object of the Cyclan.

Nequal watched them go, wondering if they would have been so eager had they known what he knew; the problem which threatened to overshadow all others. As yet it was a minor incident; but he would not have been a cyber if he had not known where it must invariably lead if unchecked.

A passage led to the laboratories; the office of Cyber Quendis, the papers and graphs lying thick on his desk.

"Master!"

"Report on the decay of the older intelligences."

Quendis was direct. "There is no improvement. The deterioration previously noticed is progressing into an increasing decay."

"Action taken?"

"The affected part of the computer has been removed from all contact with the main banks. A totally separate life support and communications system has been installed, and tests made to discover the cause of decay. Results to date show that there is no apparent protoplasmic degeneration, the condition was not induced by defective maintenance and there is no trace of any external infection."

From where he stood at one end of the Desk Yandron said, "How did you arrive at your conclusions?"

"Ten units were detached, dismantled and inspected. I chose those showing most signs of aberration."

Ten brains destroyed. Ten intelligences, the seat and repositories of accumulated knowledge, totally eliminated. Yet, thought Nequal dispassionately, it was a thing which had to be done. Again Yandron anticipated his question.

"Your suggestion as to the cause of the decay?"

"Psychological." Quendis touched a sheet of paper covered with fine markings. "The conclusions of three different lines of investigation. The cause could be based on the necessity for the brains to rid themselves of programming, by the means of paradoxical sleep. The need to dream."

"That is easily arranged," said Nequal. "There are drugs which can achieve the desired effect. Have they been used?"

"Yes, Master. The results were negative. I use the term paradoxical sleep in its widest sense. It could well be that the affected units have lost all touch with reality. This could be due to their extreme age, in which case the maintenance of units is limited by a time factor of which we have been unaware. If this is correct the decay of all units is, in time, inevitable."

"But manageable," said Yandron. "New units can replace the old."

"That is so," agreed Quendis. "Once we determine the efficient life-expectancy of the encapsulated brains, arrangements can be made for routine elimination. However the present danger lies in the possibility that the paraphysical emanations of the deteriorated units could spread the contamination."

Nequal said, "Has the affected bank been questioned?"

"Yes, Master. On seven occasions. Each time the response was sheer gibberish. The units seem to lack all coordination."

Yandron said, "Cannot something be done? The units separated and placed in cyborg mechanisms?"

"Separation has no effect." Again Quendis touched his papers, as if to reassure himself that all had been done. An odd gesture for a cyber to make and Nequal noted it. The man was more concerned than he appeared. "Rehousing the unit had no effect on the decayed intelligence. If anything it showed a marked decline. Three attempts were made. On the last the unit did nothing but scream."

Alone, distracted, terrified perhaps; torn from the close association with other minds which it had known for years. A great many years, longer by far than any normal lifetime. And yet why should any cyber scream? Certainly not from reasons of emotion. But from what else?

"Destroy the bank," ordered Nequal. "Total extinction."

"Master!"

Nequal ignored Yandron's voice, his gesture.

"Continue your investigations," he said to Quendis. "Test the entire installation down to atomic level and conduct molecular examinations of all units."

A thousand dead brains to be ripped apart and probed with electron microscopes. Tons of metal to be checked for any wild radioactivity or unsuspected crystallization. Every drop of nutrient fluid to be scanned for random chemical combinations which could have occurred, despite the monitoring devices.

And still, perhaps, they would find nothing.

As they left the office Yandron said, "Master, it could be that the decay is not from the cause Cyber Quendis suspects. The aberration could be due to the units using different frames of reference. The intelligences, old as they are, could have progressed to a higher order of relationship, using mental concepts of a type we cannot understand."

"You are saying that I may have destroyed a superior intelligence," said Nequal. "I had considered the possibility."

"Naturally, Master, but—"

"Why did I order the destruction? The answer should be obvious. If ancient brains could progress to that point then others, growing old, will reach it also. Therefore, we have lost nothing. If, however, the decay is not of that nature, then we have avoided the risk of contamination."

"Yes, Master."

Was there a hint of doubt in the carefully modulated voice? Nequal looked keenly at his aide. A man remained at the apex of the Cyclan only as long as he was efficient enough to do so. Was his aide already searching for signs of mental weakness? Questioning the destruction only after it had been ordered, so as to build evidence?

Nequal said, "There is one point which you appear to have forgotten. The affected brains were questioned and responded only with gibberish. It may be that they were using unfamiliar forms of reference, but of what use is that to the Cyclan? We deal in a world of men and must work within familiar boundaries."

Men and the problems they could cause; the normal inefficiency which grated on his desire for regulated order and logical patterns of thought.

He said, "I am returning to my office. Find Cyber Wain and join me there."

The simulacrum was in full life when they arrived, the chamber full of color, flaring greens, blues, reds and yellows; the depiction expanded so as to show a region of space in which worlds now could be revealed in multi-hued array.

Nequal stood facing it, his thin, aesthetic features painted with shifting color; the brightness accentuating the skull-like contours of his head, the mask of his face. Without turning he said, "Cyber Wain, report on your progress."

"It is slow, Master."

"Too slow."

"Agreed, but in this case time cannot be accelerated. The affinity-twin developed in the laboratory on Riano is composed of fifteen molecular units, the reversal of one unit determining whether or not it will be subjective or dominant. This we know. We also know the nature of the units. What we lack is the knowledge of the correct sequence in which they must be joined."

"And the number of possible combinations is very high," interjected Yandron. "If it were possible to try one new combination each second, still it would take four thousand years to cover them all."

"It cannot be done in a second," said Wain. He was shorter than the others, but aside from that could have been their twin. "It takes a minimum of eight hours to assemble and test a chain."

The figures were numbing. Nequal considered them as he studied the depiction. Allowing for the possibility that only half the possible sequences needed to be investigated before success was achieved, it would still take close to sixty million years. For one team, of course; more workers would reduce the figure, but still the amount was staggering.

He felt again the impatience which gripped him each time he recalled the stupidity of the guards at Riano; the willful neglect of the cybers in charge of the laboratory concerned. They had paid for their inefficiency but the damage remained. The secret of the sequence chain had been lost.

Lost, but not destroyed; of that he was certain. And what had been lost could be found again.

He said, "With the decay affecting the older brains of Central Intelligence, the matter must be moved to a higher order of priority. I have advocated this before, but my predecessor did not agree." One of the factors which had led to his replacement, but Nequal did not mention that. "The secret must be regained."

Wain made a small, helpless gesture.

"Agreed, Master, but as yet all efforts towards that end have failed. We know that the secret was stolen by Brasque, who took it to the woman Kalin. We know too that she passed it on before she died."

"To the man Dumarest," said Yandron. "Earl Dumarest. How could one man have eluded us for so long?"

For answer Nequal gestured towards the depiction, the host of glowing worlds.

"One man," he said. "Moving as a molecule would move in a heated gas. One man among billions, moving from world to world, and he has been warned. At first, when unaware he held the secret he could have been taken, had due importance been given to the matter. Now, warned, he is on his guard."

And dead cybers proved it. Cybers and agents both; those who had come close, those who had been careless. They had paid the price for underestimating the man they sought.

"The secret was used on Dradea," said Yandron evenly. "We have proof of that. It seemed that we had him fast and then he vanished."

"To appear on Paiyar and, later, on Chard." Wain was acid. "Once again we learned of his movements too late. He left on a trading vessel and now we can do nothing but wait."

"Nothing?"

Wain blinked. Engrossed in his laboratory duties he had

lost the razor-keenness of his brain; the one great attribute of every cyber had become dull through disuse.

"Master?"

"We know where he was last seen," said Nequal. "We know on which ship he left. Yandron, what is your prediction as to his present whereabouts?"

An exercise which the aide had done before, but always faced with the baffling encumbrance of random motion. One ship, moving among countless worlds, one man among so many. And Dumarest had been clever. He had not taken a commercial line which had regular ports of call. A free trader went where profit was to be found.

He said so and Nequal, without turning, gave him no chance to regain his stability.

"No motion is truly random," he said. "Even the shiftings of molecules of gas can be predicted after a fashion. And here we are dealing with a man. A clever, resourceful man, but a man just the same. And even a free trader follows a predictable path. The *Tophier* left with rare and costly oils and perfumes from Chard. Eriule would be the most probable market. They produce mutated seeds and luxury goods aimed at agricultural cultures. The probability that the *Tophier* obtained a cargo of such goods is of a high order. A prediction of 89 per cent. There are three such worlds to which they could have been taken."

The depiction expanded still more as Nequal touched the control. Now suns could be seen, worlds, satellites; dangerous proximities of conflicting energies which any ship would wish to avoid. He studied them, building on known factors, judging, eliminating; selecting the worlds on which the vessel had most probably landed, extrapolating from available data and predicting where next it would be.

An exercise in sheer intellect aimed at the one, sole object of trapping a man.

Dumarest—who held the secret which, once regained, would give the Cyclan total domination.

An exercise which had been conducted before, but which, as yet, had always failed.

Nequal sharpened the edge of his mind. From the agricultural worlds a trader would, most logically, move on to Gokan, to Narag or Guir, and then?

A moment as factors were weighed and evaluated.

"Tynar," he decided. "We shall find him there."

Chapter Two

~~~~~~

It was a harsh world with a ruby sun casting a sombre light, the air heavy with the stench of sulphur, ammonia, methane; the natural exudations augmented by the fumes from the smelters, the acrid gases rising in plumes from the pits and craters of the mines. An old world, dying, ravaged by exploiters eager for its mineral wealth.

The city hugged the field, a rambling place of raw buildings and great warehouses against which the shacks of transients clung like fetid barnacles. A nest of lanes gave on to wider thoroughfares, streets flanked with shops, inns, places of entertainment. Narrow alleys led to secluded courts faced with shuttered mansions.

A normal city for such a world, the early residents withdrawn; hating the brash newness, the greed which had shattered their peace. From barred windows they watched as the great trucks headed towards the field loaded with precious metals; the workers thronging the city eager to spend their pay. Noisy men who had brought with them their own, familiar parasites; gamblers, harlots, the peddlers of dreams, the fighters and toadies, the scum of a hundred worlds.

Seated in a corner of a tavern close to the field, Dumarest sipped slowly at his wine.

He was a tall man with wide shoulders and a narrow waist, dressed all in neutral grey, the collar and cuffs of his tunic tight against throat and wrists. He wore pants of the same, plastic material; the legs thrust into knee-boots, the hilt of a knife riding above the right. Common wear for a traveller, the metal mesh buried beneath the plastic an elementary precaution.

As was the place he had chosen, the wall which rose at his back.

A woman hesitated before him; aged, dressed in bedraggled finery, face plastered with cosmetics, eyes hard with experience. They searched the planes and contours of his face, the line of his jaw, the mouth which she sensed could so easily become cruel. For a moment their eyes met and then, without speaking, she moved away.

Another, younger, confident in her attraction, took her place.

"Hi, mister!" She smiled, resting her hands on the table and leaning forward so as to display her wares. "You lonely?"

"No."

"Just come in?" She sat and reached for the bottle, the empty glass resting beside it. "On that trader, maybe?"

"Maybe."

"Where you from?"

"Kalid," Dumarest lied. "Did I offer you a drink?"

"You begrudge it?" Her eyes, over the rim of the half-filled glass, were innocently wide. "Hell, man, are you that strapped? If you are, maybe I can help."

Dumarest lifted his own glass, touching it to his lips, eyes narrowed as he looked past the girl towards the others in the tavern. A motley collection of spacemen, field workers, pimps and entrepreneurs. None seemed to be paying him any attention.

"I can help," repeated the girl. "You've a look about you—you've been in a ring, right?"

"So?"

"I can tell a fighter when I see one. If you're broke I could arrange something. Ten-inch blades, first cut or to the death. Big money for a fast man if he wants it. I've a friend who could line it up if you're interested."

He asked, knowing the answer, "Is there much of that going on?"

"Fights?" She shrugged. "Plenty, but you'll need a guide to the big money. You don't want to be cheated. Why don't I call over my friend and let him make the proposition?" Without waiting for an answer she turned, mouth opening as if to shout a name. It closed as Dumarest leaned forward and closed his fingers about her wrist.

"What the hell!" She stared at the clamping hand. "Mister! You're hurting me!"

"We don't need your friend," he said flatly. "And I don't want company."

"Not even mine?" She smiled as she rubbed her wrist, the marks of his fingers clear against the flesh. A mechanical grimace, as if she had remembered to play a part. "You're strong. Damned strong. And fast; I never even saw you move. You'd be a joy to watch in a ring. How about it, mister? We could make a deal. My cut wouldn't hurt you."

"No," he said dryly. "But it could hurt me."

He saw by her expression that she didn't understand. To her the fights were a spectacle to be enjoyed, something by which to make a profit; but to those engaged it was something far different. Dumarest leaned back, remembering; the bright lights, the crowd, the stink of oil and sweat and fear. The smell, too, of blood; and the savage anticipation of those who watched others kill and maim, to cut and bleed and die for their titillation.

It was always the same. In an arena open to the air, where men fought in the light of the sun; or in some small back room filled with shadows, the risks were the same. A slip, a momentary inattention, an accident, a broken blade or a patch of blood; all could bring swift and painful death. Only speed and skill had saved him, that and luck—and who could tell how long that luck would last? Already, perhaps, it had run out.

"Mister?" He felt the touch of her hand, saw the puzzled expression in her eyes. "Did I say something wrong?"

"No." He moved his hand away from her touch. "But you're wasting your time."

"So what? It's my time." But even as she shrugged, she had turned to look at the others. "Nothing," she said, reaching for her glass. "Let the others have the pickings—those old crows need it more than I do. Anyway, it makes a change to talk. What's your name? Where are you from? How long have you been on the move?"

Too many questions from a harlot who should be intent on business; watched, probably, by a ruthless pimp who would not be gentle. And there were more.

"Did you really come in on that trader? When are you pulling out?"

He said, "Drink your wine."

"You don't want to talk?"

"No."

"Well, it's your business." She refilled her glass and

drank half at a gulp. "How about a different kind of a deal then? You and me—you know?"

"I told you you were wasting your time."

"I've a nice little place close to here. We could get some food and I'd cook you a meal. You'd like that. I'm a good cook and it wouldn't cost you all that much. We could sit and drink a little and eat and talk, if that's all you want. How about it, mister? I'm not that bad for a man who wants company."

She was trying too hard, wasting too much time, and it didn't fit the pattern of her kind. There could be others like her in every tavern, more in the hotels; a host of watching eyes. He felt the prickle of warning which had so often saved him before, the primitive caution reacting to the possibility of a trap.

It was time to move.

Rising he dropped money on the table; enough to pay for her time, to save her from a beating if she was exactly what she appeared to be. A cluster of men stood at the bar and he circled them at a safe distance. The door was low, forcing him to duck as he stepped into the street.

Outside, they were waiting.

It was almost dark, the great ball of the sun a sullen glow on the horizon; the street filled with smoky shadows patched with blobs of luminescence from windows and lanterns set behind tinted panes. In such light details were lost; but Dumarest could see the hulking patch of darkness to his right, another to his left, a third facing him from across the street. Loungers, perhaps, casual wanderers or some of the familiar predators of the night; the thieves and muggers always to be found in such places, pimps offering the bodies of their women.

But such men would not work in harmony, would not all ease forward at the same time, their pace accelerating as he moved from the low doorway.

Three of them at least, and others could be within easy distance.

Dumarest stopped, rose, knife in hand; a beam of stray light catching the nine-inch blade, winking on the honed edge, the needle-sharp point. Even as he drew the knife he had turned, was running back the way he had come, past the doorway of the tavern towards the man who loped towards him.

From behind came an urgent voice. "Get him!"

The man was tall, lithe, a fighter with accustomed reflexes; hampered now by his clothing, the unexpected speed of the attack. Even so he was fast. As Dumarest lunged forward he backed, lifting his hand, something whining from the weapon he carried.

Dumarest felt it rip at his shoulder as he ducked and then he was on the man; knife lifting in a blur, the edge biting, dragging through the flesh and bone of the wrist so that hand and weapon fell in a fountain of blood. Even as the man opened his mouth to scream the point was rising, slashing to hit the throat, to sever the arteries feeding the brain.

"Mineo!"

Dumarest spun at the sound of the voice. The man at his rear was close, the one opposite halting as he raised his gun. At a distance of forty feet he thought he was safe, taking his time as he aimed. He took too long. Even as he aligned the barrel Dumarest was moving, his arm lifting; the knife was a shimmer as it lanced through the air to bury its point in an eye, the brain beneath. Unarmed he leapt to one side, forward as the remaining assailant hesitated, undecided whether to fight or run. The delay cost him his life. Even as he fired Dumarest was on him; the stiffened palm of his right hand cutting at the side of the neck, the fingers of his left gripping the hand which held the gun, crushing flesh against metal. Again he struck, felt the impact, heard the dull snap of bone and turned; poised as a man came running down the street towards him.

"Earl! What goes on?"

Branchard, the captain of the *Tophier*, the vessel which had brought Dumarest to Tynar. He pursed his lips as he saw the dead; watching as Dumarest recovered his knife, wiping it clean on the man it had killed before thrusting it back into his boot.

"Earl?"

"They were waiting for me. There could be others."

"Then we'd better get out of here." Branchard scooped up a discarded weapon. "Let's go!"

They found a place in a small inn towards the center of the town; a discrete place with a troupe of dancers moving gracefully to the tap of a drum, gossamer fabrics catching varicolored light so that they seemed to move in a kaleidoscope of subtle luminescence. The wine was worth less than a tenth of what they paid, but the price was for entertainment and privacy. In the glow of an emerald lantern, Branchard examined the weapon he had found.

"A dart gun," he commented. "Vibratory missiles which throw the central nervous system all to hell. They can cripple, but rarely kill. Whoever was after you, Earl, didn't want you dead. Robbers, maybe?"

"Maybe." Dumarest looked at his shoulder. The plastic was torn, the mesh beneath bright. Unable to penetrate, the missile had left him unharmed.

"But you don't think so." Branchard was shrewd. "You could be right. Three men, armed like they were; it doesn't make sense. One would have been enough, but I guess they wanted to make sure."

Dumarest said, "I waited. What kept you?"

"I had trouble finding Eglantine."

"And?"

"I found him," said Branchard heavily. "Earl, you're crazy. His ship's a wreck. If you want to commit suicide there are a hundred more pleasant ways. Listen," he added urgently, "there's no need for going off like that. Stick with the *Tophier*. We're doing well, mostly thanks to you, and we can do better. Why waste all you've made on chartering a vessel which won't be able to hold air for much longer, let alone get where you want it to? Why not use the *Tophier*? Hell," he said dryly, "we can use the trade."

"Where are you heading when you leave Tynar?"

Branchard shrugged, "It depends on what we can get as cargo, Earl. Maybe Lochis with metals, or Hemdalt with stones. Branch, even if we can get nothing but local products. Anywhere which will show a profit. You know that."

"Yes," said Dumarest. "And so do others."

"Those after you?" The captain frowned. "I've not asked, Earl, because it's your business. I figured that if you wanted me to know you'd have told me. But I can guess. You've got powerful enemies, right?"

Dumarest nodded.

"And I can make a guess that they are fond of wearing scarlet. That's why you had to leave Chard in a hurry. Well, no matter; as it turned out they did me a favor. Now I want to do you one. To hell with profit. Give the word and I'll take you anywhere you want to go. I mean it, Earl. Anywhere."

For any captain to make such an offer was rare, for a Free Trader unknown. Dumarest poured Branchard more wine.

"Thank you, but no."

"Why the hell not?"

For reasons Dumarest didn't want to explain. Already he had stayed with the *Tophier* too long; but the last port of call had been bad as regards easy shipping, the one before even worse. Now they had found him; the city was alive with potential enemies and, once they learned of the cargo the ship would be carrying, any cyber would be able to predict where it would next land. And that would not be necessary. Already the ship would have been planted with detectors, arrangements made to negate any plan of escape he might have considered, using the ship as a vehicle.

He said, "If I leave with you we'll be followed. Burned out of space, maybe. You want to risk that?"

Branchard glowered at his wine.

"Well?"

"No, Earl. I'll be honest. The *Tophier* is all I have. Once it's gone I'll be no better than a stranded traveller. But would they really do that?"

"They'd do it."

For the sake of the secret he carried. The correct sequence of units which formed the affinity-twin. The means by which one mind could dominate another, to the extent of literally taking over mind and body. To use a subjective host to gain a new existence; to see and taste and feel, to enjoy a completely new life. A bribe no old man could refuse, no aging matron resist.

"All right, Earl." Branchard accepted defeat. "You'll do as you think best, but I still think you're crazy to ride with Eglantine. What else do you want me to do?"

"Nothing." Dumarest looked towards the stage. The dancers had gone, replaced by three women who sang like angels; the thin, high notes of their song rising like the sigh of wind, the thrum of harps. "Just be honest. Make a point of telling people what you're carrying and where you are going. Someone will ask for passage—give it to him. If anyone asks about me, tell them the truth. I've shipped out, but you don't know where. Tell them about Eglantine if they press. Remember that you've got nothing to hide. nothing to answer for."

And, if he was lucky, nothing would happen to him or his vessel. He would be watched, followed perhaps; checked for a while and then forgotten as no longer being of importance. Forgotten—and safe.

Branchard finished his wine.

"So this is it, Earl. Goodbye. I guessed it would have to end. Do I have to tell you that, anytime we meet, you've always got a friend?"

"No," said Dumarest. "You don't have to tell me that."

"We'd best leave together. I'll go out the front door and you take the one next to the stage. It leads to a back alley. Turn left and climb the wall. Go right and you're heading towards the field. Eglantine is expecting you." Branchard blew out his cheeks. "Look after yourself, Earl."

Eglantine was small, fat; his face creased like a prune, his eyes twin chips of agate, his teeth startlingly white. His ship was like his clothes; patched, worn, soiled with stains.

"Earl Dumarest." He gestured to a chair in the dingy room used as a salon. "Branchard told me about you. You want to charter the *Styast*, right?"

"You know it."

"But the terms of charter were a little vague. And, as yet, I've seen no money."

"The terms are what I say." Dumarest was curt. "Ten thousand ermils to the next planetfall."

"Which will be?"

"Where I say after we have left Tynar." Dumarest jingled the money; thick, octagonal coins each set with a precious gem, accepted tender on any world. "If you've changed your mind say so now. There are other ships."

"But none as cheap," said Eglantine quickly. "And, perhaps, none available. But let us not be hasty. All I know is that you want to charter my ship. To the next planetfall, you say; but that could be a world on the other side of the galaxy. Where's the profit in that? A man has to know what he's selling."

"And buying," snapped Dumarest. "From what I hear your vessel is a wreck. Maybe I'm making a mistake."

"Maybe," Eglantine shrugged and spread his ringed hands. "What man can claim that never in his life, has he made a mistake? And yet why should we quarrel? You need my vessel and I am available. All I ask is for a little information. What cargo will you be carrying?"

"None."

Eglantine hid his surprise. No cargo, which meant that Dumarest was in a hurry to get away and had no wish to travel on a normal ship. Charters were never cheap, but had certain advantages; and why should he object when the money was in plain view? Yet old habits died hard. A man willing to pay so much might be pressed to pay even more.

Then he looked again at the man before him, and changed his mind. In any game of bluff Dumarest would be the winner. In any confrontation he would never lose. There was that look about him, the hard sureness of a man who had never known the protection of House, Guild or Organization; who had early learned to rely on no one but himself.

But still he had to assert his position; as captain he was in command.

"Our destination," he said. "I must know it. Surely you can see that."

"As I said, you will be told it after we leave."

"That will be tomorrow at sunset."

"No," said Dumarest. "It will be now. Is your crew aboard? They should be. It was part of the deal. Now let's get down to it. Is the ship mine or not? Make up your mind."

Eglantine said, "I expect you would like to examine the crew."

Like the ship and the captain, the crew left much to be desired. An engineer with a blotched and mottled face, who reeked of cheap wine and had a withered hand. A handler, a boy; star-crazed and willing to work for bed and board, filling in as steward. A navigator, with rheumed eyes and a peculiar, acrid odor which told of a wasting disease. And a minstrel.

He looked up from where he sat on his bunk, as Dumarest looked through the door. Like the captain he was fat; unlike him, he had a certain dignity which made his soiled finery more of a challenge to an adversary than the outward evidence of laziness. A stringed instrument lay on his lap; a round-bellied thing with a delicate neck and a handful of strings which he was busy tuning. A gilyre of polished wood and inset fragments of nacre, once an expensive thing; now, like its owner, the worse for wear.

"Arbush," said Eglantine. "He plays for us."

"And gambles," said the man. He had a deep, pleasant voice. "And sings at times; and tells long, boring tales if it should please the company. And tells fortunes and reads the lines engraved in palms. Once I saved the captain's life. Since then he has carried me around."

Charity which Dumarest would never have suspected from the captain. Or perhaps it was not simply that. Like the boy, the minstrel was cheap labor.

He touched the strings of his instrument, and a chord lifted to rise and echo in the air.

"A song," he said. "Which shall it be? A paen or a dirge? Young love or withered discontent? Something to lift your heart or to throw a shadow of gloom over the spirits? Name it and it will be yours."

Dumarest caught the edge of bitterness, the hint of mockery. An artist reduced to the status of a beggar. If he was an artist. If the gilyre was more than just show.

"Later," said Dumarest. Outside, in the passage, he said to Eglantine. "Call the boy."

He came, wary, his eyes wide in his thin face, his attitude betraying the beatings he had suffered; the desperate need to swallow his pride in order to remain where he wished to be. Dumarest waited until they were alone and then drew coins from his pocket.

"There is a ship on the field, the *Tophier*. Find it. Tell the captain that I sent you. He will give you a place on his vessel."

"You're kicking me out?"

"I'm not taking you with me. This ship isn't fit for a man, let alone a boy. Here." Dumarest gave him the money. "Buy yourself some food and decent clothing. Buy a knife and learn how to use it. Learn to walk tall."

"But the captain?"

"To hell with him," said Dumarest evenly. "He's using you, you must know that. I'm offering you a chance to find a decent life. Take it or not—that's up to you. But you don't ride on this vessel."

Nor, if he had the sense, on any other like it; but only time could give him that. Time and the luck which would enable him to survive. At least he had been given his chance.

He turned as the boy scuttled away and heard the thrum of strings. Arbush, silent, had come close and must have heard. But his face, creased with the lines of cynicism, held none of the mockery Dumarest had expected to see.

"An unusual gesture," he said above the soft blurring of the strings; a muted succession of rippling chords which could be used to accompany a song or a conversation. "I do not think our captain will be pleased, yet I think the boy will live to thank you."

"I didn't do it for thanks."

"No, but for what? A wish, perhaps, that someone had treated you the same? Or as a recompense for a good deed received in the past?" The strings murmured louder. "Or were you simply trying to save him from destruction?"

Dumarest said, flatly, "I'm riding on this ship. It's my neck as well as yours. Or would you prefer to leave?"

"To what? A corner in some filthy tavern? My songs bartered for bread? I have known that, and know, too, that here I am better off. A bed, food, company of a kind. And more. Perhaps the thing for which you are looking. The thing all men seek. Happiness? Who can tell?"

A romantic, a soiled visionary; or perhaps a creature lost in the mists of deluding drugs. Symbiotes could do that, giving mystic images in return for food, warmth and safety; repaying their sometimes willing hosts in the only coin they possessed.

"Eglantine sent me to find you," said Arbush. "He is ready to leave. Shalout itches to set the course. You have met him?"

"The navigator."

"Exactly. Once he was an expert at his trade, now he is not what he was." Arbush shrugged. "Are any of us? Yet he can guide us from world to world, given time. Time and coordinates. The first he has; the second you are to give him."

"Later," said Dumarest. "When we are well into space."

"And so he is to send us into the unknown," mused the minstrel. "Sending the five of us, like a hand, hurtling into the void. A fist to hammer the face of creation. A poetic concept, as I think you will agree."

"I think that you talk too much and say too little."

"Perhaps." The eyes in their folds of fat moved a little, became a trifle more hard. Anger? If so he mastered it well. "And perhaps you talk too little and say too much. There is a message in silence. Fear, maybe. Distrust certainly. Yet you do not appear to be a man ruled by fear. Caution, then? If so, how can I blame you? In this life we all walk on the edge of extinction."

A philosopher of sorts as well as an artist, the fingers which strummed the gilyre were deft with practiced skill. Dumarest studied them, noting the tell-tale callouses, the splaying of the tips. The fingers and other things; the set of the rotund frame, the position of the feet, the tilt of the head. Men were not always what they appeared to be; but, as far as he could tell, Arbush was not one of them.

And, even if he was, it was too late to alter his own plan.

"And so we leave," said the minstrel softly, the music from the strings rising a little, taking on a sombre beat, a pulsing rhythm. "As legend has it that men of old first left their place of birth. To venture into the empty dark with nothing but hope as their guide. Shall we find El Dorado? Jackpot? Bonanza? A new Eden? Camelot? Worlds of mystery and untold wealth lying like jewels among the stars; lost planets or worlds that are nothing more than the figment of dreams. Is that what you seek?"

The music rose, loud, imperious, blended chords interspersed with vibrant tones; a strange, disturbing melody carried over the throbbing strum of the accompaniment, a masterly demonstration of skill.

It roared, softened, rose to fade again to a stirring whisper, against which the resonant voice of the minstrel echoed like an organ.

"On such a trip as this who knows what might befall us? Life? Death? Riches or poverty, space holds them all. Those who search must surely find. Happiness. Contentment. Paradise itself, perhaps." The strumming grew louder, harsh chords rising above it, reaching a crescendo, falling with startling abruptness into silence. A silence in which echoes whispered from the walls, the floor, the roof of the passage.

A whispering vibration against which the organ-like voice, muted now, had the impact of a sharpened spear.

"And, who knows, perhaps even Earth itself!"

Chapter Three

Eloise had taken special care, setting out a tray of tiny cakes, crisp things adorned with abstract designs and bright with touches of color. Another tray bore goblets of fine crystal placed close to decanters of sombre red and vivid blue wine. The liquids of forgetfulness, thought Adara bleakly. Forgetfulness and a false courage; the poison which numbed minds and made even the prospect of imminent conversion a bearable concept. Protection against what was to come. A defence for himself at least, though the woman did not seem to need such aid. He glanced at where she sat, lounging in the deep chair at the far side of the room; the curtains drawn back from the window at her side to reveal the city beyond, the spires and pinnacles, the rounded domes, the streets and buildings which stood in their mathematically precise arrangement, coldly white beneath the pale glow of the stars.

She said, "If the sight bothers you the curtains can be closed."

"No." He dragged his eyes from the window. "It does not bother me."

"Not the darkness? The cold?"

Shaking his head he looked directly at her, studying her as he had done a thousand times before; more conscious now than at any time before of the influence she had had on him, the way in which she had altered his perception. Conscious, too, of her beauty which sat framed in the arms of the chair.

She was tall, thin fabrics covering the long, lithe lines of her figure; the material enhancing the swelling contours of hip and thigh, the narrowness of her waist, the twin prominences of her breasts. Her neck was slender, her face strong with finely set bone; the eyes deep, watchful beneath thick and level brows. Tonight she had dressed her hair in a rising crest which exposed the tiny ears, the gems at their lobes, more gems glittering in the ebon mane. The nails of her high-arched feet naked in thin sandals were painted a flaring crimson; the color matching that on her fingers, her lips.

Hard as he searched he could find no trace of the trepidation which surely must possess her, the mounting dread which threatened to engulf him.

An animal, he decided, and envied her the cool self-possession which clung to her like a cloud. A strong, female animal who should have borne many children—he was disturbed by the train of thought. In Instone, such things were not the province of those who lived under the aegis of Camolsaer.

Camolsaer!

It was all around, everywhere, watching, calculating, omniscient—inescapable!

He felt the sudden dryness in his mouth and looked longingly at the wine, yet the formalities had to be observed.

Stiffly he said, "My thanks, Eloise, for your invitation. This is not a good time to be alone."

"Then why suffer it?"

A question which she had asked before, many times; and to which, as now, he could find no answer. Because it had always been so. Because things did not change. Because instilled pride maintained the composure which was a part of his heritage. Why were her questions so direct? The answers so difficult to find?

Weakly he said, "You are a stranger. You would not understand."

"A stranger?" The musical resonance of her voice held an acid amusement. "You say that, after so long?"

"You were not born here."

"True, thank God. But does that assume a lack of comprehension?" She rose as he hesitated, the thin fabrics she wore streaming behind her as she stepped towards him; the scent of her perfume signalled her proximity. "Adaral My friend!"

Their hands touched, softness against softness, the delicate fingers no harder than his own. Her body too, he knew, held a more than equal strength. Once it had disturbed him; now there was no time or room for concern. And yet he was grateful for her presence.

His hand shook a little as he reached for the wine.

"So soon, Adara?"

"You deny me?"

"Nothing—I owe you too much for that. But do you think it wise?"

"You tell me that. You provided it."

"To celebrate."

He lifted the lambent fluid trapped in its container of crystal and looked at the vivid blueness. One glass would do no harm. Two even and, if things went against him, what did it matter how much he swallowed? And he needed the strength it could lend.

"To celebrate," he said, mocking her tone. "To show my gratitude? To what? The Goddess of Luck you have so often mentioned? You see, my dear, how you have corrupted me. In this place there is no such thing as luck."

"Nor guts either, from what I've seen!" Immediately she was contrite. "I'm sorry. You can't help being what you are and, God knows, I've little cause to berate you. It's just that, at times, I—"

"Will you join me?"

"No." She had sensed the raw emotion within him, the turmoil which could be controlled only by an effort. "Drink if it pleases you, my friend. Drink and be happy for tomorrow we die."

Only the wine stopped the words; the savage, biting words which sprang from the outraged core of his being. For her to have so broken all accepted convention, at a time like the present!

The goblet rang a little as he set it down, its rim barely touching that of another, producing a thin, high note of ringing clarity.

He didn't look at the woman as he stepped towards the window.

Outside the streets were deserted as he had known they would be. Now everyone was inside, warm, seeking what comfort they could; those with the low numbers having already accepted their fate and engrossed with a final enjoyment of the flesh, or sitting in solitude doubting their ability to maintain their composure.

But not all of them. Some would be surrounded by friends, the center of attention, drinking with careless abandon or lost in the euphoria of drugs; the need of careful abstinence thrown aside like an outworn garment.

He said, his forehead tight against the coolness of the pane, "How long?"

"Not very long now." He scented her perfume as she moved towards him, felt the soft weight of her hand on his shoulder. "Adara—you are not alone."

Words, comforting perhaps, but what did they mean? What else was he now but alone? Who could share his torment, ease it by taking a part of it from him? Like physical pain, it had to be borne. Like the dreams which had ruined his sleep, the sickness he had felt when on his way to this very room.

"Adara?"

Irritably he moved away from the hand on his shoulder, stepping back from the window a little, unwilling for her to see his face. A soft face, older than he remembered; the eyes shadowed pits as they stared at him from the reflection in the crystal, the muscles lax with lack of self-control. Yet control must be maintained. Tradition and pride demanded it. Self-respect if nothing else. And still it was hard.

Harder still when he remembered the incident which had happened while on his way to join Eloise.

A small thing, but it had shaken him. He had passed two Monitors in the passage and the sight had turned his knees to water so that, for a long time, he had leaned against the wall lacking the strength even to stand. An odd thing to have happened. All the years he had lived, it had never happened before. But then he had never drawn so low a number before; had never appreciated the full significance of what he had seen.

"Adara!" The musical voice was urgent. "Turn, look at me! Adara!"

As he obeyed the great bell began to toll.

It was a sound which filled the city, dominating, imperious, a deep, solemn throbbing which came from the very walls, the air itself; causing little harmonics to quiver the panes of the window, to set the goblets trembling so that they touched and filled the air with singing chimes.

At the third knell he began to tremble; a hateful reaction which constricted his stomach and caused tiny muscles to jerk along the line of his jaw, the apparatus of his hands. Desperately he hid the discomfiture, keeping his face a blank mask; aware of the woman, her eyes, his own growing terror. The tolling continued, each knell a claw raking at his naked brain.

". . . six . . . seven . . . eight . . ."

Eloise had regained her chair and sat, watching him with a peculiar intensity. Almost, he thought wildly, as if she were studying a specimen to determine how efficient its training had been. Relentlessly her voice kept time to the bell, counting the strokes; merging with the sonorous throbbing, the thin chiming of the goblets which now sang with a rising note as if the inanimate material could sense and respond to his mounting distress.

". . . eleven . . . twelve . . thirteen . . ."

He felt perspiration dew his forehead, the body beneath his clothing; the trembling now increased so that he had to lock his fingers to disguise their rebellion. To remain detached. To remain calm. To accept what had to come. The teachings of a lifetime— why had they failed him now?

". . fifteen . . . sixteen . . sev -"

"Eloise?"

"Sixteen, Adara! Sixteen!"

Her voice was a shout of triumph filling the room with gladness and, he thought, relief.

Relief which in no way could equal his own. "Are you certain?"

"Listen!" Her upheld hand demanded silence. All around, the walls seemed to retain the tolling note of the bell so that ghost-echoes quivered in the air and tricked the senses. Yet there was no substance to the sound. It was nothing but a ghost lingering in his own brain, whispering in his ears.

"Sixteen, Adara! You were number eighteen and I was twenty-two. We're safe! Safe!"

His hand trembled as it reached for the wine. Red or blue, did it matter? Yet red was the color of blood, and blue of hope. Now there was no need of hope. Ruby liquid spattered as he shakily poured it. A man reborn, reprieved. The wine slid down his throat as if it had been water, his goblet refilled before the woman had lifted her own.

"To life," she said.

"Eloise!"

"To life," she repeated doggedly. "And to hell with conventions which insist that no one must speak of life or death, or the crazy pattern of the city in which we're stuck. To hell with the city. To hell with Camolsaer!"

"You're drunk!" he shouted. "Drunk or mad!"

"Not drunk, Adara. And not scared. The bell has tolled, remember? The choice has been made. Those poor, damned fools who lost have gone to their living hell. Gone, or on their way. So drink, you fool, and enjoy life. Enjoy it while you can."

She drank, throwing back her head; the slender length of her throat fully exposed, taut, lovely. With an abrupt gesture she threw aside the empty glass so that it shattered into fragments against the wall and then reached towards him, hands extended, eyes enormous with emotion.

"Eloise!"

She stepped closer; her mouth wide, sensuous, the lips full and softly moist.

"No!" He backed, cautious, afraid.

"You coward!" Her voice, still musical, now held the chill of contempt. "Afraid to drink too much. Afraid to break things. Afraid even to make love too often. Terrified even to talk about life and death, and what happens to those who have lost. Fear. Is that what rules you? Are you so in love with it that you can't remember what it is to be a man? Have you ever known?"

"Eloise! Please!"

Camolsaer would be watching, noting; measuring the emotional content, the amount drunk, everything. He saw her hands come towards him, the fingers curved, light reflected from the points of her sharpened nails. They touched his cheeks and he felt the stab of incipient pain, yet could do nothing to prevent her stripping the flesh with her talons if she so desired.

And then, abruptly, she dropped her hands.

"Reaction," she said huskily. "It hits people in different ways. Let's get the hell out of here."

The city was at gruesome play. A long conga line of near-naked men and women wound down the passages, past the adornments, beneath the arched roofs and down the ramp into the main assembly hall. There, at the far end, a man stood between two Monitors. At least he seemed to be standing and then, Adara saw that he was being supported at each side, his feet hanging inches above the floor.

"Larchen," said a man at his side. "Number four. He tried to put a good face on it, but collapsed and tried to run. A bad thing to have happened."

"And Thichent?"

"As you'd expect. He drew the prime and knew there could be only one end. He left the party at the first knell; an example to us all." He smiled at Eloise, bobbing his head. "You look superb, my dear, but then you always do. A little wine?"

"Aren't you afraid of Camolsaer?"

"After the bell there is always a period of grace. Didn't Adara explain that? Drinks taken now are not counted. A concession for which we must be grateful. But surely you know this?"

She had known it, realized Adara sickly. It had been himself who had forgotten. Or perhaps not forgotten, but distrusted. The woman's fault—why had he ever saved her?

Taking the proffered glass she said, quietly, "Chol, you amaze me."

"In what way, Eloise?"

"In your acceptance."

"Of what?" He frowned, genuinely puzzled. "Things are what they are—what they have always been. We are born, we live, we leave. It is as simple as that."

"Leave?" Her voice was faintly mocking. "Don't you mean that you die?"

Flushing, he said in a high voice, "Now listen, I know that you're a stranger, but that is no way to talk. You've been here long enough to have learned our customs. We don't—die." He seemed to gag on the word. "We are converted."

"Yes," she said.

"Changed! Improved!" His voice was now almost a scream. "Thichent knew that. He realized and accepted it. He was proud to be the first. To pay his debt to the city, to us, to Camolsaer."

"Who are you trying to convince?" she said flatly. "Me or yourself?"

"Adara!"

Adara answered the appeal, taking her by the arm and guiding her away from Chol, the others who had overheard. Beneath his fingers he felt the quivering of her flesh, the anger which threatened to consume her. A pair of girls ran towards them, long streamers of bright fabric in their hands, the material breaking beneath his impatient gesture. Pouting at their spoiled pleasure, they ran towards others more receptive of their attention.

"Eloise, why be so foolish?"

"You call it that?"

"To upset Chol and the others, yes."

"To upset them?" She shrugged. "To teach them, you mean. To try and reach them. To stop them from being so blind."

"To spoil their pleasure." His voice was brittle with impatience. "Have you learned nothing? To talk as you did was stupid."

"Stop it, Adara."

"But—"

"Stop it!" She pulled her arm free and turned to face him. Colored light from drifting globes bathed her face with shadowed radiance, accentuating the structure of the bone, hardening the contours in their rigid anger. "I won't be lectured by you or any man in this insane city. Nor any woman. If you want to know why, just look around. Minutes ago they heard the bell. Now every damned fool acts as if he were at a party."

"It's custom, you know that."

"Madness!"

"No." He reached for her arm and felt a momentary hurt as she avoided his hand. "You are disturbed, but that is natural. I understand. But it is all over now. There is no need for concern. You, I, both of us are safe."

"For how long?" She gave him no time to answer. "Until the next draw," she said bitterly. "The next selection. How can you be sure that you won't draw prime? And, if you do, will you walk willingly to your death as that fool Thichent did?"

"Please, Eloise."

"Death," she repeated savagely. "Death, damn you! Death!"

She saw the sudden pallor of his face, sensed the abrupt hush from those who had overheard; the tension, the shifting away from where she stood. Afraid, all of them, herself too; but with a fear more corrosive than their own. They were simply afraid of what she said; she was terrified of what the future could hold.

"Eloise!"

Adara stepped towards her, one hand extended—he, at least, displayed a little courage. But not enough. Not anywhere near enough. And, now that the bell had tolled and the danger was over, old habits would regain their hold.

Rabbits, all of them, men and women both—and she, dear God, was trapped among them.

"Eloise!"

She turned as Adara touched her, running through the assembly; passing startled faces and barely conscious of the voices, the laughter, the gaiety which ruled beyond her immediate vicinity. A winding stair led to the summit of a tower and she reached it, pressing open the door; walking to where a high parapet edged the city, the area beyond.

Tiredly she leaned against it, barely aware of the chill which numbed her flesh through the thin clothing, the harsh pressure against her breasts.

The night was still. Here, in the cup of the valley, was little wind; but higher, where the ringing hills stood like pale sentinels, their slopes and summits thick with ice, there would be a frigid blast whining from the north, carrying particles of snow and sleet; a killing wind which robbed body-heat and brought killing hypothermia.

She remembered it, her skin puckering at the memory. A bad time in which she almost died. Should have died, she thought bleakly. At least, then it would have been over.

"Woman Eloise, it is not wise to stand here dressed as you are."

Engrossed with memory she had heard no sound and, as always, the Monitors were silent on their padded feet. She turned, looking at the thing. Seven feet tall, a body made of articulated plates, limbs, torso; all in a parody of the human frame. The face too, cold, hard despite the paint, the eyes elongated curves of crystal. Starlight shone on the figure in a cold effulgence, accentuating the chill of the night.

"Woman Eloise, you must return below."

The voice was like the body, cold, flat; an emotionless drone.

"No. I—"

"Woman Eloise, you must return."

She could argue, try to run, but the end would be the same. She could walk or be carried like a stubborn child, but the Monitor would be obeyed.

Always the Monitors were obeyed.

It followed her down the stairs, halting as she entered the assembly room, watching as she thrust her way into the crowd, to the passages leading to her room. The fragments of the glass she had shattered had vanished; another goblet replacing the one broken, clean and bright on the tray.

She filled it with lambent blue wine and drank and refilled it with ruby, they carried it over to the window where she stood looking out over the city, upward to the stars.

A host of suns, the vault of the sky filled with glittering points, sheets of luminescence, patches of nacreous light, the blur of distant nebulae.

Suns around which circled a multitude of worlds on which men could walk free. Ships traversing the gulfs between them. The ebb and flow of restless life of which once she had been a part.

The glass lifted in a silent toast, a prayer and then, abruptly, she collapsed in a storm of weeping.

Chapter Four

Branchard had been right—the *Styast* was a wreck. The plates were worn, the hull leaked air, the control room a mass of patched and antiquated equipment, the engine room a disgrace.

But it was a ship in space and would have to serve.

Alone in his cabin Dumarest studied a scrap of paper on which were written the spacial coordinates of Tynar. Others were beneath them, the course they were now following, figures chosen by throwing dice. He threw them again, noting their value, using the figures shown to write a new set of figures.

A random selection impossible to predict. A means to send the *Styast* to a point the Cyclan could never anticipate.

He would throw again and then send the vessel to the nearest, busy world. A place from which he would move on to hide among the stars.

To hide and to continue his endless search.

Outside the cabin the ship was still. In the engine room Beint, the engineer, would be busy with his wine, slumped before his panel; the withered hand resting on the console beneath the flickering dials and flashing signal lamps.

Arbush was in the salon, an immobile figure frozen over his gilyre. Eglantine was asleep, a gross mound on his bunk; unaware of the cautiously opened door, its gentle closing. Shalout was in the steward's quarters, standing like a statue before the medical cabinet, vials before him, a hypogun in his hand. Like the minstrel he was immobile, caught in the magic of quick-time; his metabolism slowed to a fraction of normal so that, to him, an hour seemed but seconds.

A good time to do what had to be done.

In the control room Dumarest looked around. Beneath the screens bright with clustered stars the instruments clicked and whispered, as they guided the vessel through space. Touching the metal he could feel the faint but unmistakable vibration of the drive, the Erhaft field which drove them at a velocity against which the speed of light was a crawl.

The supra radio was where he had expected it to be.

He stooped, fingers turning the clamps, drawing out the instrument to expose the inner circuitry. A tug and a component was free. Another and the instrument was ruined unless there were replacement parts, and the possibility of that, on the *Styast*, was remote.

Back in the corridor Dumarest took a hypogun from his pocket, checked the loading and lifting it, aimed it at his throat. A touch of the trigger and quick-time was blasted through skin, fat and tissue into his blood. The lights dimmed a little and small noises became apparent. The thin, high sound of a plucked string, discordant, shrill. A clinking, the sound of indrawn breath.

Shalout busy with his medications.

He turned as Dumarest approached, sweeping a litter of vials back into their boxes, slamming the door of the cabinet as if ashamed at having been seen. The acrid odor he carried was accentuated by another, sharp, sweet; the stench of drugs to combat his infection, a fungoid growth picked up on some too-alien world.

He pursed his lips at the figures Dumarest gave him.

"Are you serious? Do you realize just where these coordinates will take us?"

"Just set course so as to arrive at that point."

"A long journey, Earl. Too long for the *Styast* to make. We haven't the supplies, even if the vessel would stand it. The captain—"

"Just do as I say," interrupted Dumarest. "I may give you another set of coordinates later."

Shalout said, shrewdly, "You are taking a random path, is that it? Are you afraid that someone could be following us? If they are, we won't be able to shake them."

"But you can tell if they are there."

"True," admitted the navigator. "The scanners would pick up the emissions of their drive. But they could have more efficient detectors than we carry." For a moment he

stood, frowning, then shrugged. "Why do I concern myself? You have chartered the ship and have the right to
dictate where it is to go. But if I could have a hint, a clue;
I·could, perhaps, shorten the journey."

Dumarest said, softly, "Do you know the way to
Bonanza? To Earth?"

"Earth?" The navigator frowned. "Why should a planet
be called that? Earth is dirt, ground, loam. All worlds
have earth." Then his face cleared and, smiling, he said,
"You have been listening to Arbush. His greeting song, as
he calls it. A plethora of exotic names and hinted mysteries. Once, I believe, he worked on a tourist vessel and old
habits die hard. Bear with him long enough and you will
be tempted to follow him into a region of dreams. Non-
sense, of course, but it beguiles the time."

"And Earth?"

"Does not exist. A myth which has risen from who can
guess what reasons? The desire for a paradise, perhaps; a
longing for a world in which there is no pain, no suffering,
where all things are possible and all men are heroes. Another legendary world to add to the rest. You mentioned
one, Bonanza. There are others, all equally legendary.
None has substance."

Dumarest knew better, but he didn't press the matter. It
was just another hope lost; another dead-end to add to the
others.

He said, "The coordinates?"

"Our course is to be changed." Shalout looked again at
the figures. The drugs he had taken had cleared his eyes a
little from their rheum, had given him a false buoyancy.
"What would we find if we followed these figures to the
end?" he mused. "Would any of us be alive at the end of
the journey? Would we find a world in which thoughts became things and a dream became reality? Is there such a
world? Or would we find ourselves in a region torn and
blasted by opposing forces, our generators ruined, the hull
burst open, ourselves turned into radiant energy? Beings
still aware, but freed of the confines of the flesh? An enticing concept, my friend, as I think you will agree."

The more so for a man dying of a foul disease, living
on the euphoria of drugs, the charity of a captain.

Dumarest said, patiently, "The coordinates."

"Of course. I have ridden too long with the minstrel.
His romancing has affected me; at times I even find myself

using his words. Once, on Zendhal I—but never mind. A man should not dwell in the past. Yet it is true that Arbush seems to have a wealth of odd scraps of information."

"Of Earth, perhaps?"

Shalout shrugged. "That you must ask him."

He sat where Dumarest had last seen him, crouched over the table in the salon, busy with his gilyre. Frowning he tuned the strings, listened, tuned them again, plucked a rill of chords and impatiently pushed the instrument away.

"Useless," he said as Dumarest joined him. "The notes are too shrill, too high. Quick-time has its blessing, but the enjoyment of music is not one of them. You wish to play?"

"Later."

"Your fortune, then."

"It has been told before."

"But not by me." Arbush reached out and took Dumarest's right hand, turning it so as to study the palm. For a long moment he concentrated, the fingertip of his free hand tracing the lines, their conjunctions. "Were you a woman I would use flattery and the older you were, the more I would use. Promises of loves to come and riches to be gained. Good health and stirring adventures of the heart. Instead I—"

He broke off, leaning closer, a subtle change coming over him so that the mask of banter turned into a thing more serious.

"You have killed, Earl, often; that I can see. There is much blood on your hands. Blood and sadness and great loss. An unhappy childhood, a lonely time; and there are long journeys made under the shadow of extinction."

Travelling Low, doped, frozen, ninety percent dead, lying in caskets meant for the transportation of beasts; risking the fifteen percent death rate for the sake of cheap transportation.

The converse of High, in which the use of quick-time eased the tedium of the longest journey.

Dumarest said, dryly, "Now tell me something I do not already know."

"The future?" Arbush glanced up, his eyes intent. "There is danger, that is plain. Relentless enemies and—other things."

"Such as?"

"Death. With you it is very close. A familiar companion. And luck, more than your share. I think it would be wise to reconsider my invitation to play."

"Then let us talk." Dumarest pulled his hand free from the other's grip. "Tell me what you know of the Original People."

A veil fell across Arbush's eyes. "I do not understand."

"You mentioned them. The men of old who left the planet of their birth. You want the pure source?" Dumarest's voice deepened to hold the rolling echoes of drums. "From terror they fled, to find new places on which to expiate their sins. Only when cleansed will the race of Man be again united."

"An intriguing concept, Earl, but obviously a barren one. How could all the peoples of the galaxy ever have lived on one world? Think of the numbers, the differences, it doesn't make sense."

"A world can be populated by a handful of settlers," reminded Dumarest. "And mutations could have caused the changes."

"True, but—"

"Terra," said Dumarest softly. "Another name for Earth. Tell me about Earth."

"A legendary world."

"So Shalout told me. I think you know better. How did you learn of the name? Why make a point of mentioning it?"

"For effect." Arbush leaned back, his eyes clear, calm in his composure. "The fabric of a song, no more. A device to titillate the sense of adventure. I picked up the name— somewhere, I forget just where. The fragment of legend also. Perhaps at a lecture I attended when young. Something overheard from a private conversation. Sit in any tavern and your ears will be assailed with rumours." He reached for a deck of cards. "Shall we play?"

"Later."

"I have disappointed you, but that cannot be helped. Ask what I know and the answers are yours. How Beint hurt his arm, for example. You have seen the engineer's hand. He was careless one night and was attacked in a dark alley by someone who carried a poisoned blade. The nerves are gone."

"The damage could be repaired."

"True, a regrowth, obtained on any decent world—with money, Earl. Beint does not have the money." Arbush turned over a card, the jester. Quietly he added, "He would do a lot to get it."

"And Shalout?"

"Beyond hope by now. The fungoid is eating itself into his brain. But he could spend what remains of his life in luxury—if he had the money."

"And you?"

Arbush turned over another card, the lady. He followed it with the lord. "Men, women and fools," he murmured. "And which one is you? Not the woman and not, I think, the fool." Riffling the deck he said, blandly, "Shall we play?"

The cabin had a door which didn't fit; a lock which now, for some reason, failed to work. The ventilator carried sounds of metallic impact, an off-center fan or one with a broken blade; sound enough to disguise the whisper of voices. Dumarest listened, then jumped down from the bunk to the floor. On the cot lay the hypogun he had already used; his system normal, the effects of quick-time neutralised.

When they made their move, he would be ready for them.

And the move would be made, the message had been plain. Arbush, for reasons of his own had betrayed the captain, reenforcing Dumarest's own suspicions. A wreck of a ship, a man who obviously wanted to hide, the hints they could have picked up on Tynar—the *Styast* had become a trap.

A trap which was about to close.

Dumarest heard the scuff of boots in the passage, a sudden sonorous chord, a muffled curse in Eglantine's voice.

"Tell that damned minstrel to be quiet!"

An order to Shalout, perhaps, but Beint would be the better choice. Hampered by his withered hand, he would be of less use in a struggle. Not that Eglantine expected one; as far as he knew Dumarest was locked in quick-time, a helpless prey.

In which case, why move now?

The radio, he decided. Eglantine had tried to use it and found it ruined. It would stay ruined, the components had been destroyed; no word could be sent ahead as to his coming.

Dumarest eased open the door.

Outside the passage was empty. If Beint had gone to join Arbush in the salon, then Shalout must be towards the right at the end of the passage leading towards the engine room. And Eglantine?

He caught the scrape of movement, the shift of air; he spun, one hand dropping towards the knife in his boot, the hand freezing as he saw the captain, the laser he held in one pudgy hand.

"Hold! Move and I fire!"

The gun was steady, the muzzle aimed low to sear legs and groin, the knuckle white over the trigger. A fraction more pressure and it would vent its searing beam; energy to burn clothes, skin, muscle and bone. To cripple if it did not kill.

Dumarest said, blankly, "Captain! Is there something wrong?"

"Shalout! To me!"

The knuckle had eased a little, no longer white; the captain more certain of his command of the situation. He stood in a cabin, the door barely open; the gap just wide enough to show his face, the weapon he held. As the navigator came running down the passage from the engine room Eglantine said, sharply, "That's close enough. Watch him. Burn his legs if he tries anything."

Shalout, like the captain, held a laser. He halted, twenty feet from Dumarest.

He said, puzzled, "He's riding Middle like the rest of us."

"Yes." Eglantine opened the door wide and stepped into the passage. "Proof of what I suspected, if I needed proof at all. Why should an honest man suffer the tedium of a journey when there is no need?"

Dumarest said, "Your drugs are old, Captain. They lack effectiveness. I woke and was riding Middle. I was about to obtain more quick-time from the cabinet. Now, perhaps, you will tell me what is wrong."

"The radio is ruined. You must have done it. Where are the components?"

"You need guns to ask me that?"

"They could be in his cabin," said Shalout. "Shall I search?"

For a moment Eglantine hesitated, then shook his head. He had the advantage and wanted to retain it. With the navigator in the cabin he would be left alone with Dumarest. "No. He will tell us where they are." The laser moved a little, menacing. "You will tell us."

Dumarest said, "Here?"

The passage was narrow, with an armed man at front and rear; he would be caught in the cross fire if he tried to attack. In the salon, perhaps, he would stand a better chance, even with Beint present. Arbush would, he hoped, be neutral if not an ally.

As if the man had caught his thoughts the sudden thrum of a gilyre rose from the compartment to send echoes along the passage; a stirring, demanding sound, hard, imperious.

A voice rode with it, bland, more than a little mocking.

"Are we to be left alone, my friend? Were you sent here to keep us out of the way? Does the *Styast* now carry two crews, when it used to carry one? Are secret deals being made and fortunes promised? If the trap has been sprung, where is the victim?"

Eglantine shouted, "Arbush! Shut your mouth!"

As the gilyre fell silent, Beint loomed at the end of the passage.

"So you've got him," he rumbled. "Good. Bring him in here so we all can listen to what he has to say."

He backed as they passed, his withered left hand tucked into his belt, his right holding a short club of some heavy wood. It made little slapping sounds as he struck it against his thigh. Arbush sat on the table, the gilyre on his lap, blunt fingers idly stroking the strings; tapping the wood so as to produce a soft thrumming interspersed with the whisper of simulated drums.

He said, "Captain, you could be making a mistake."

"No mistake," snapped Eglantine. "The radio proves that. Why should a man want to ruin the instrument?"

"Why did you want to use it?" Dumarest looked at the round face, the splintered glass of the eyes. "What need did you have for it? And why was I not told? Do you forget that I chartered this ship?"

"I am the captain!"

"And a thief. You took my money and reneged on the deal. Why?"

Eglantine shrugged. He was more relaxed now, the laser hanging loose in his hand, confident of his mastery.

"A man wanting to charter a ship for a single passage. A man without cargo who is willing to pay highly for the privilege. You could have bought High passage on a score of ships for what you paid. And then your demand we follow a random course. I asked myself why? Are you interested in the answer?"

"Tell me."

Let the man talk; while he did so he would relax even more. And his words would hold the attention of the others, reassuring them of their anticipated wealth. And, while he talked, it was possible to plan.

Dumarest moved a little, so as to rest the weight of his hip against the table. Shalout would have to be saved, his skill would be needed. Beint also; the engines needed constant attention if they were not to drop from phase. Abrush was an unknown factor; as yet he had shown himself to be a friend, but it would be a mistake to rely on him and he was expendable.

As was Eglantine.

Any ship was lost without its captain, but emergencies happened and Eglantine was a poor specimen of his kind. The condition of the *Styast* proved that. Without him it would be possible to reach their destination, and all navigators held a basic skill. Shalout could do what had to be done if Eglantine were to die.

And the man had to die.

Dumarest altered his position a little more as the captain talked, proud of himself, his conclusions.

"Ten thousand ermils," he said. "A healthy sum, but a man worth that could be worth much more. And a man does not run without cause. Then I remembered things I had heard on Tynan. A reward offered—need I say more?"

Dumarest said, "Why not? Are you afraid the others will know as much as you?"

"We share! It is agreed!"

"Share—how much? The little you choose to give them?" Dumarest shrugged, casual as he shifted position once more; edging along the table so as to narrow the distance between himself and the captain. "Or perhaps they trust you. Rely on your word—as I did!"

"You—!"

Dumarest moved, muscles exploding in a burst of controlled energy; the knife lifting from his boot as he neared the captain, thrusting as the gun lifted, catching the laser in his left hand to turn as the dead man fell, the hilt of the knife prominent over his heart.

"Drop the gun! The club! Do it!"

He fired as they hesitated, wood smoking, the club falling as Beint snatched away his hand.

"Shalout! Don't, you fool!"

The navigator dropped his gun at Arbush's shout. He looked dazed, numbed; eyes wide as he looked at the dead captain, the pool of blood in which he lay.

"Fast!" said the minstrel. He had not moved from where he sat. "I've never seen a man move so fast. Once you had the gun, you could have killed us all. Why didn't you?"

"I need you," said Dumarest harshly. "Beint, get to the engines. Shalout, you—"

He broke off as the lights quivered. A shrill hum came from the bulkheads; a thin sound, rising, penetrating, hurting the ears. Abruptly the ship seemed to twist in on itself; the edges of the compartment turning into curves, the bulkheads into corrugations.

"Dear God!" screamed Shalout. "We're in a warp!"

Chapter Five

~~~~~~~~~~~~~~~~~~~~~~~~~~~~~~~~~~

Somewhere a sun had died, matter imploding, condensing; torrents of energy hurled into space, agglomerations of incredible forces which distorted the very fabric of the continuum. For eons, perhaps, they had drifted; some to be caught in the gravitational well of other suns, to destroy them in turn or to be absorbed if weak enough. Some had touched planets and left them charred cinders. Others had merged with alternate patches of drifting energies, to conglomerate into areas in which normal laws did not apply.

The *Styast* had touched one.

"A warp!" Shalout screamed again. "We're dead!"

Dumarest stepped forward, lifted his hand, sent the palm hard against the navigator's cheek. Twice more he struck; stinging slaps which shocked the man from his hysteria.

As the rheumed eyes cleared a little he snapped, "To the controls. Fast!"

He led the way, the ship jerking again as he ran down the passage: the walls seeming to close in, so that he looked down an edged tunnel which seemed to extend to infinity. He ran on, not looking down at his legs, his feet, the soft squashiness of the floor. And then it had passed and the passage was normal again; the instruments in the control room were a flashing, clicking mass of confusion.

The screens showed madness.

The stars were gone, the sheets and curtains of luminescence, the sombre patches of dust and the glowing nimbus of distant nebulae. Now there was a riot of color; swathes of green, red, yellow, savage blue, all twisting in dimensions impossible to follow, changing even as the eye caught them to adopt new, more baffling configurations.

"We can only barely have touched," said Dumarest.

"Shalout, check to see where the core lies. Change course to avoid it."

The room changed before the other could answer, the walls expanding, filled with eye-bright luminescence; the instruments changing into cones, cubes, tesseracts of brilliant crystal, rods of lambent hue. The mind and eye baffled by the impact of wild radiation, trying to make sense from distorted stimuli. Or an actual, physical change in which familiar items altered to fit new laws of perspective and construction.

No man had ever lived to determine the truth.

Dumarest dropped into the control chair as the room returned to normality. Beside him Shalout muttered as he checked his instruments, reading dials he no longer trusted, readings which carried little sense.

"There, I think, Earl. No, there!"

"Make up your mind!"

"I can't! The sensors are all gone to hell. Earl!"

Dumarest was not a captain, yet he knew something about ships. He had ridden in too many, worked in more, not to have learned something of what needed to be done. Seated in the chair, he gripped the controls. To turn the *Styast* needed delicate manipulation of the field. Lights blazed on the panel as he adjusted the levers and a dial flashed an angry red.

"The engines. They're losing phase. Damn Beint for a drunken fool. Arbush, see what you can do!"

The minstrel had followed them. He turned at the command and headed towards the engine room. Dumarest didn't see him go. Every nerve, every particle of his concentration was aimed at the controls.

Again he adjusted the levers. The screens flared, changed, showed the familiar universe.

"You did it!" Shalout babbled his relief. "Earl, you did it!"

"Maybe." Dumarest wasn't so sure. "We could have barely touched an extension of the warp. We must have, or we could never have pulled out of it."

And they weren't clear yet. Other ships had suffered narrow escapes, still more were lost after reaching apparent safety. Dumarest looked at the instruments, the scanners and sensors which should have guided them safely through space. Would have done, had Eglantine been at his post in order to read their warnings. Yet, per-

haps, he could not wholly be blamed. A warp distorted all
space in its immediate region. Instruments would have
been delivering false information, and yet, a trained and
skilled man might have been able to avoid the trap.

"Shalout?"

The man remained silent, shaking his head, a thin line
of spittle running from the corner of his mouth.

"Shalout, damn you! Give me a course!"

The man changed. His arms vanished, his legs, his head
became a truncated pyramid of gleaming facets; his body
a mass of divergent angles glowing with red and blue and
emerald. Beyond him the metal of the hull sprouted frost-
ed icicles, the instruments soft and pouting faces.

Again the screens showed nothing but a lambent confusion of writhing brilliance.

And then, again, things returned to normal.

"Dear God!" The navigator had found his voice. "We're
trapped! We can't escape! We're dead!"

Ship and men, the vessel caught in a malestrom of irre-
sistible forces, swept like a chip of wood caught in a
tumultuous stream; to be ripped and torn and crushed to
individual molecules.

If the force was resisted.

It was natural to resist, to use the relatively minor
power of their engines to pull away, to escape if there was
a chance. But the engines of the *Styast* were almost useless, hovering on the edge of becoming lifeless lumps of
metal and wire; ready to collapse and take with them the
Erhaft field which was their life.

Dumarest said, tightly, "Get hold of yourself, Shalout.
We've still got a chance. See if you can determine the flow
of the warp, its node."

"But—"

"Do it!"

For a moment the man hesitated, a victim of his terror;
then he remembered the dead man lying in the salon, the
blood, the knife which had reached his heart. Saw the
hard, set line of Dumarest's features, the cruel line of the
mouth.

Death would come, of that he was certain; but death
delayed was better than death received at this very moment.

He studied his instruments, checking, noting; hard-won
skills diminishing a little of his fear.

"Up and to the left," he said. "If these things can be trusted that is the direction of flow. Not that it means anything. Who can tell what happens in a warp? But you asked and that's the answer."

"And the node?"

"Anywhere. Directions don't mean anything."

"Try harder."

"Ahead, maybe. How can I tell?"

With instruments which could lie and eyes which couldn't be trusted—no way at all. Yet his instinct remained. That and luck.

As the screen flared again with the alien brilliance, Dumarest sent the vessel up and to the left. Towards the line of flow, riding with it instead of resisting it; sending the chip which was the *Styast* moving inward closer to the heart of the warp, the node it must contain.

At the sound of the bell Eloise woke to face yet another day. They were all the same, days and nights; segments of time divided by a bell, different only in the external light. Hours which brightened to fade, to brighten again. A sun which rose and set; the steady, relentless passage of time. The inescapable end—but it was best not to think of that.

Rising she bathed and dressed, a serviceable garment of dull green, more like a sack than a dress; but in the gardens, frills had no place.

For a moment she hesitated and then decided to eat alone; the canteen would be full of the usual vacuous faces, the empty chatter. Here, in her room, at least she could maintain the illusion of privacy.

Of the three choices she chose toast, fruit and a compote of pungent flavor together with a sweet tisane. The fruit was genuine, the compote a blend of mutated yeasts; the tisane a synthetic combination balanced as to essential vitamins and trace elements.

A meal containing the three essentials of any diet; bulk, variety and flavor. Camolsaer looked after them well.

A Monitor stood at its usual place, at the entrance to the gardens.

"Woman Eloise, you are three minutes late."

"So what?"

"It is noted. Proceed to bank 73. Remove all dead matter and observe for infection."

Yesterday it had been bank 395 to harvest the fruit, or

to overseer, rather; machines did the work. And the day before that, it had been to replant bank 83. And last week she had worked in the kitchens. And the week before that at the laundry. Simple tasks all, any of which could have been done by an idiot.

She said, "My application to the nursery. Has it been approved?"

"It has been noted."

"I said approved."

"It has been noted," droned the Monitor again. "You are now six minutes late. Proceed at once to bank 73."

It was a wide, long, shallow tray filled with grit to hold the roots, nutrients to feed the plants. From above fell light rich in ultra-violet, and from speakers came a jumble of sound, vibrations designed to promote optimum growth.

Eloise walked along the edge, picking wilted leaves, dropped particles; fragments of vegetation from where they broke the symmetry of the growths. God working in his garden, she thought bitterly. But it was not a real garden; the work was trivial and she certainly was not God.

A woman lower down moved slowly towards her. As she came into earshot Eloise said, "Doesn't all this get you?"

The woman frowned. "What do you mean?"

"All this." Her gesture took in the tank, the wide expanse of the gardens. "We don't need it. The yeast and algae vats can supply all we eat. Flavor and shape can be added, so why all this?"

"It's for Camolsaer."

The answer she had expected and wondered why she had bothered. It was always the same. A lifetime of conditioning couldn't be negated by a few conversations. With an effort, she remembered the woman's name.

"Haven't you ever thought about it, Helen? I mean, all this wasted effort. We aren't really needed here."

"That isn't for us to decide, Eloise." The woman carefully plucked a leaf and dropped it into the bag she carried for later disposal. "But one thing is clear. I like to eat fruit, nuts and vegetables, so they have to be grown. If they have to be grown, then someone has to grow them. Who else but ourselves?"

The cold logic of a machine.

Eloise moved along the bank searching, for want of anything better to do, for signs of rust, blight, infection of any kind. She found none, as she had expected. When next they drew nearer to each other Helen said, "I've made application for nursery duty. It has been approved."

"When?"

"I start tomorrow. I—"

"When did you make the application?" Eloise was curt, careless of her interruption. Anger thinned her lips at Helen's answer. "I applied long ago. Before you did. I'm still waiting."

"I'm sorry." Helen looked into her bag. "Perhaps, well, you did act rather oddly after the Knelling. And it could be that—"

"I'm irrational," snapped Eloise. "I'm emotional. I'm not to be trusted. So your precious Camolsaer is making me pay for it." A plant fell to ruin beneath the grip of her hand. "Damn it, Helen, what can I do?"

But she knew the answer to that. To work hard, be humble, be stable; to forget that she had known a life outside of Instone.

To patiently wait and to die—no—be converted with a smile.

Another plant pulped to ruin, a third, and then the Monitor was at her side; the hateful voice droning above the susurration from the speakers.

"Woman Eloise, you are disturbed."

"Yes."

"Your reason?"

"I want something. It has been denied me."

"Your application has been noted, as you were told. Is there something else?"

"Yes, I—" She looked around at the gardens, the massed vegetation, the blank faces of those busy at their tasks. "I'm an artist. I don't belong here. I want to do something more creative."

"You are relieved, Woman Eloise. Report to the medical center for tests and examination."

The doctor was a robot, its attendant a man. He read the printout and thoughtfully pursed his lips.

"There is clear evidence of inner conflict, Eloise. Physically you are in perfect condition, but the mental symptoms are disturbing. Of course I realize that you are a stranger; but you have been here long enough to have be-

come assimilated into the culture of Instone. Is there anything I could do to help?"

"I want to be with the children."

"Of course. Natural enough for any woman, and you
have a strong survival index which means a highly developed maternal instinct. If it were possible for you to
have a child, it is probable that your inner tensions would
be resolved."

Quickly, too quickly perhaps, she said, "No. I don't
want a child. Not here."

"Then that is one conflict which need not concern us."

He had missed her meaning. "What else is left? The
monotony of essential employment? Perhaps something
could be done about that. Have you any special prefer-
ence? The engraving of glass, for example; or, at least, the
fabrication of designs for ornamentation? You did say you
were an artist."

"Not that kind."

"Well, then, let us probe a little deeper. Clothing is
standard for work, of course; but that worn during leisure
hours is capable of wide variety. Would you be interested
in fashion? Or perhaps . . ."

His voice droned on, but she wasn't listening. Seated in
the chair, the attachments of the robot diagnostician hanging like a skein of hair before the cabinet, she berated
herself for having been a fool.

How many times must she remind herself to foreswear
the luxury of emotion?

A score of times, at least, she thought dully; and now
she had done it again. Anger was always futile, a self-in-
dulgence which achieved nothing aside from the alienation
of friends. Outside it was bad enough; here in the city it
was toying with suicide. Did she want to die?

An escape, she thought bleakly, but the final one. And
she couldn't be sure that it was an escape at all. It could
be the preliminary to something worse than she had now.

And, while there was life, there was hope.

Where had she heard that? Sitting, her hands lax in her
lap, she threw her mind back to the past. A tavern, or a
place like it. A man, a little the worse for drink, who had
thrown a handful of coins at her feet. A dying man with a
seared face and lungs which vented blood when he
coughed. But stubborn, fighting to the last, refusing to
take the black pill the medics had offered.

"Eloise?" The attendant was looking at her, a frown creasing the smooth skin of his forehead. "Is there anything wrong?"

"No." With an effort she smiled. "I am sorry, but I was thinking. I have acted very foolishly."

"You realize that?" His relief was obvious. "That is good. Once a problem is accepted and faced, then it can be resolved. We are all prone to tension, it is a part of the human condition; but such tension can be negated by an acceptance of reality. Here, in Instone, you are fed, housed and protected. In return, you work at things which have to be done. A fair exchange, as I think you will agree."

"Yes."

"The very act of living is a demand. A universal concept which cannot be denied. Organisms must die to provide your body with sustenance and, as you make demands, so demands are made of you. To grow food, to maintain the city, to cooperate in order to survive."

Repetition which, even when she had first heard it, had created a vague disquiet. Life was more than just living. A child born should do more than just grow, live, pass on. That was the destiny of animals, not men.

She said, slowly, "Life is a continual act of violence."

"Yes," he admitted. "I suppose you could put it that way. On the animal level, certainly; but we are more than animals."

"Are we?"

A question which disturbed him. Sharply he said, "You doubt it?"

"No." Already she had skimmed too near the edge. Continue and there would be drugs, more tests, observation and discussion. It was time to end her dangerous play. "I feel better now. Talking to you has done me a great deal of good. I was upset, disturbed, my thoughts unclear. The Knelling—you know how it is."

"It disturbed you?"

"There were friends, people who were close; it is foolish, I know, but I was afraid."

"And now?"

"Not now." Was anger fear? Frustration, terror? "I have made mistakes," she admitted. "I regret them. I shall not bother you again."

"It is no bother, Eloise. I am here to help. Call on me

at any time. And now, I suggest that you take up some therapeutic activity for a while."

"Thank you."

"A moment." He stepped back beyond her range of vision and she heard a soft hum, the murmur of voices. Returning he said, "Corridor 53. Continue the refurbishing."

Adara stretched, feeling the muscles tighten across back and shoulders, dropping his hands in time to catch the heavy ball thrown at him by one of the others in the ring. Bikel was spiteful, hurling the hard mass of plastic with savage force, smiling a little as Adara fumbled the catch.

"You're getting old," he said. "Maybe you should give all this up?"

Old, perhaps; but not so old that he couldn't hold his own in the gymnasium. Adara hefted the ball, feinted, sent it with the full force of his arms and shoulders to where the man stood. He heard the grunt as the hands slipped, the meaty smack as the ball hit the other's stomach, and felt a warm satisfaction.

"Not bad," said Sagen. The instructor had smooth skin, unbulged by overdeveloped muscle. He lifted his hand as Bikel poised the ball, the throw. "That's enough for now."

"Let's continue."

"No. Exercise as much as you want, but not with the ball." He had sensed the rising antagonism. "Into the pool now, all of you."

The water was deep, green, ringed by naked figures. Adara dived, swam underwater until his lungs felt like bursting, then surfaced with a mist of spray. The exercise had stimulated him and he reveled in the joy of the moment. A couple to one side dived, swam and rose laughing, the girl lifted on the man's hands; water dripping from her hair, the uptilt of her breasts.

Vivien and Dras, selected for breeding, soon to have a child.

The thought ruined his pleasure and he swam to the side, to heave himself up from the pool.

Rhun called to him as he dressed.

"We're having a challenge match tonight, care to join in?"

"I don't think so."

"Two teams at multiple chess. The losers to pay forfeit."

"No." Adara had no interest in the movements of pieces on a board, the pitting of his intellectual skill against that of others. Still less in the ridiculous penalties demanded of the losers. "Some other time, maybe."

"Think again, Adara. Bring Eloise with you. She could enjoy it."

Mention of the name brought a touch of guilt. He had been avoiding her, he realized; not consciously, but with an instinctive caution. Impulsively, he strode to a terminal.

"Adara. Where is Eloise?"

Without hesitation came the answer. "In her room."

She was wearing a dress of orange laced with streaks of brown; green paint on lips and nails, her hair a rippling waterfall over the smooth roundness of her shoulders. Her eyes widened at the sight of him.

"Adara! How did you know I was thinking about you?"

"Were you?"

"Of course, my friend. Who else in this place is as close? Some wine?"

A decanter stood on a low table, next to the deep chair which had been turned so as to face the window. The curtains were withdrawn, the darkening blue of the sky already showing the cold points of stars. She had, he guessed, been sitting, brooding; and he felt a momentary shame.

"Eloise, I'm sorry."

"For what, being careful?" Shrugging she lifted a glass half full of wine. Green wine, he noted, chosen, perhaps, to match her lips. "I'm dangerous, Adara. Bad company. Others know it, so why not you?"

"No!"

"Yes," she corrected. "At times I go too far. Today, I was sent to the medics."

"And?"

"Nothing. I realized that I was wrong and said so. Camolsaer gave me a job refurbishing a corridor."

To revive old paint with new. To set fresh pigment on faded designs; work which required no skill, but did need concentration.

She said, "There was a place on my home world where they did things like that. Set people to make mats or weave tapestries on a loom. Insane people. Adara, am I insane?"

"No!" His protest was almost a shout. "No," he said again, more quietly. "You are not insane and never think that you are. Your values are different from ours and that is all."

"All?" She shrugged. "What else is insanity but a different set of values? An inability to accept what the majority regard as the norm? Tell me, my friend, when I use the words 'breaking point,' do you know what I mean?"

"The point at which any material, under stress, can no longer resist the pressure."

"Or the pull of opposing forces."

"Yes. You are precise, my dear."

"I'm a fool." She poured him wine and handed him the glass, refilling her own and gulping it down. As she again tilted the decanter she said, "I'm drinking too much, but what the hell? Might as well be hung for a sheep as a lamb."

"Your analogy escapes me."

"As do so many other things."

He said, to change the subject, "I saw Vivien and Dras in the pool. They're going to have a child."

"I know."

"And Rhun asked me to bring you to the chess match. He made a point of it."

"So?"

"You still have friends, Eloise. You're not alone."

"That is a matter of opinion." Immediately she softened. "I'm sorry, Adara, I know you and the others mean well, but—why the hell can't you understand?"

A question he had asked himself many times in the years he had known her. He had tried and, at times, imagined that he had succeeded. Then, as now, she would change into something almost alien.

He reached towards her where she stood, turned away from him, her face towards the window. Her hair was soft with a delicate sheen; yielding tactile pleasure to his questing hand, his stroking fingers.

"Adara!"

His hand fell from the tresses, a coldness at his heart, but she hadn't rejected him.

It was something else.

High in the sky something glowed; a cloud of vivid

blue, bright against the darkening night. A lambency which flickered, died, flared again as it swept across the heavens.

"A meteor," he said. "A big one, by the look of it. It should land fairly close."

"A meteor?" Her voice rang high, excited. "Hell, that's no meteor! It's a ship!"

Chapter Six

~~~~~~~~~~~~~~~~~~~~~~~~~~~~~~~~

There were clicks, sighs, the rasp of yielding metal; a host of tiny sounds which had replaced the grating roar, the crush and fury of destruction. Dumarest heard them all around, a whispering threnody which echoed in his ears; fading even as he listened, to die with solemn murmurs. The dirge of a dying ship.

He tried to move and felt clamping restrictions. Opening his eyes he stared at the black faces of the screens, the material scarred and splintered in a cobweb of lines. Weight dragged him sideways and he realized the control room was tilted; what had been the deck was now a wall to which the chair was fastened.

For the moment it was enough.

He sagged, breathing deeply, conscious of the ache in his chest; ribs bruised or broken by the straps which held him. His lips and chin were wet and sticky with blood which had come from burst capillaries, the vulnerable cells of his nose. His head throbbed and he felt as if he had been beaten all over with clubs.

But he was alive.

Incredibly, he was alive!

After a while he moved, one hand lifting to hit the release; the straps opening to spill him onto the side of the hull which was now the deck. A short fall but one which sent spears of agony through his chest; which caused bright flashes to fill his vision. The corner of some broken instrument had dug into his temple, and fresh blood ran down his face to join the rest.

And it was cold. Cold!

The sting of it was like fire, the metal under his hands burning with frigidity. The air itself stung as he breathed it, the sharpness acting as a spur. Again he moved, turning, rising to his knees, to slip and fall with one hand outstretched.

It landed on something soft; a ball with contours and convexities. A face.

Shalout was dead.

He lay, a crumpled heap against the instruments which had once been his charge. His mouth was open, saliva thick on his chin; the eyes open and filled with the consuming terror he had known. The head lolled at a peculiar angle, the neck broken, death reenforced by the impact which had crushed the lower side of his skull.

Rising, Dumarest caught the tilted shape of the chair to steady himself. Crystal grated beneath his boots as he made his way to the door, the passage beyond. That too was tilted, frost gleaming on the soiled metal, the vapor of his breath a plume carried before him.

Stumbling, slipping, he crawled towards the steward's room, to the medical cabinet it contained. By a miracle the door had not sprung open; instead it was jammed. He tore at it with his bare hands, then, remembering, made his way to the salon.

Something had ripped open the side admitting frigid air, and a pale luminescence which accentuated the weak glow of the indestructable emergency bulbs. In it, the body of Eglantine looked like a discarded bundle of rags tossed into a corner; rags stained with blood and internal liquids among which he found his knife.

Back at the cabinet, he thrust the blade into the crack of the jammed door and heaved. Sweat dewed his face, metabolic heat combating the cold as he strained against the hilt, fighting the waves of pain which threatened to engulf him. A snap and the door was open, the knife falling as he searched what it contained. Vials of drugs, a hypogun, old and with poor calibration; antibiotics, some instruments, plastic sprays, hormone-enriched dressings, and a small box containing what he wanted.

With numbed fingers he loaded the hypogun and fired it three times, into his neck.

Relief was almost instantaneous. Dumarest straightened, taking a deep breath, careless of the damage shattered ribs might be doing to internal tissues. It was enough for now that the drugs had killed his pain. With the reflex of old habit, he picked up the knife and slipped it into his boot.

Then it was time to examine the ship.

The *Styast* was ruined, that he had known. Somehow the impact of landing had twisted the foremost part in a ninety degree angle, breaking the structure just beyond the salon to leave the rest upright. At the point of strain the hull had ripped open to reveal a dully shining wall of ice, a jagged prominence thrusting its way into the vessel, a heap of splintered fragments almost reaching to the roof at the far side of the break. Brushing them aside, Dumarest jerked open the door and made his way to the engine room.

Like the rest of the ship, it was a ruin.

Globules of metal made bright sparkles on the floor, the inner components of the generators which had failed just before impact; released energies fusing the interior and venting it through the ripped casings in showers of molten rain.

Beint was dead, his face plastered on the panel, his withered hand outflung in a mutely appealing gesture.

Arbush was still alive.

He lay at one side of the room, his bulk trapped beneath a clutter of metal, a beam nipping his rotund bulk. His eyes were closed, a thin rim of ice crusted on the fabric of his blouse, the jagged edge of torn metal inches from his face.

As Dumarest touched his cheek he opened his eyes.

"Earl!" he whispered. "Thank God—I thought I was alone."

"Can you move?"

"No. I've tried. The crash knocked me out, I guess, but I wasn't out for long. At least I don't think so."

"Try again."

Arbush tensed, the effort mottling his face; then relaxing he said, "It's no good, Earl. It feels as if my back's broken. If it is—"

"You'll die easy," promised Dumarest. "But let's make sure."

Rising from where he knelt he threw aside scraps and sheets of metal, pipes and the essentials of the life-support apparatus, the bulk of a ventilator. The beam was a main stanchion, thick and heavy, creasing the body where it held the minstrel. Dumarest gripped it at the upper end and strained.

"Move!" he panted. "Use your arms to crawl, if that's all you can do."

The weight was too much. He felt the room begin to spin as he struggled against the inert mass, a roaring begin to fill his ears. In his mouth there was the taste of blood.

Like a crippled spider, Arbush inched himself over the floor.

"Hold it, Earl," he gasped. "Let it go now and it'll snap my spine."

"Hurry!"

Dumarest grunted as he felt the weight begin to slip from his hands. With a final effort he threw it to one side, away from the crawling figure. With a crash it slammed to the floor.

"Arbush?"

"I'm all right." The man was standing, wincing as he flexed his legs. "The damned thing must have hit a nerve when it fell. Paralyzed me for a while and then held me fast. It was a bad time, Earl. All I could do was to lie there, not knowing if anyone else was alive; waiting to starve, to die of thirst and cold." He shivered. "A hell of a way to go."

"There are worse."

"Maybe, but if so, I don't want to hear about them." Arbush pursed his lips as he studied his companion. "You look in a hell of a state."

Dumarest caught at the console to steady himself. The final effort had robbed him of strength and the plump figure of the minstrel seemed to swell and shrink before his eyes.

He said, "My ribs could be broken. Get drugs from the medical cabinet and something to bind my chest. You'd better hurry; we've a lot to do."

There was food, some basics which had escaped spilling, and other things. Sitting in the salon they ate; sipping the sickly compound, heavy with glucose, laced with vitamins and flavored with citrus, a cup of which provided energy enough for a day. Eglantine's cabin had held succulent dainties; soft meats and spiced fillets of fish, compounds of nuts and honey, fruits steeped in spirits. They ate regardless of choice, using the food as essential fuel; a means to combat the cold.

They had chosen the practical clothing they wore, thick layers of assorted garments tightly bound with straps and thongs.

Raking the final fragment of meat from a tin, Arbush threw it aside and gave a gusting sigh.

"I've eaten worse and I've eaten better, a dozen courses served with wine by a smiling wanton; but never have I enjoyed a meal more."

Dumarest made no comment. He was stiff, his torso tightly bound with dressings, his blood thick with drugs. He had washed the blood from his face, neck and hands and treated superficial abrasions; but a little of the ache remained despite the medications. And nothing could ease the situation.

"We were lucky," said the minstrel somberly. "We had more luck than anyone could deserve. To be trapped in a warp and escape from it—"

He broke off, shaking his head, thinking; remembering the time of madness when all familiarity had vanished and nightmare reigned. The chaos as the ship had travelled into the warp, riding a tide of fury to the very node itself; protected only by the Erhaft field, the whine of the laboring generators.

There was no way to tell how long it had lasted. A second, a year; both could have been the same. And then to be spat out like a pip between closing fingers; to be thrown into a region of normal space at incredible velocity so that, abruptly, a world had loomed before them.

He said, again, "We were lucky."

Luck which hadn't lasted. The generators had failed as they neared the ice, the ship falling, to be sent hurtling down an icy wall, to hit a crevasse; to be ripped and torn apart as, within, soft flesh met unyielding metal.

An impact which Dumarest had been unable to avoid.

He said, dryly, "Maybe the others were the lucky ones."

"No, Earl, you know better than that. For them it is over, true; in the gamble we made they lost as we won. Had Shalout been at the controls, none would have survived. As I told you, Earl, you have more luck than most. I read it in your palm."

"Is that why you sided with me?"

"Did I?" Arbush raised his eyebrows. "Well, maybe I did. A hint to an intelligent man is better than a book to a fool. And maybe I have old-fashioned ideas about the keeping of bargains. Well, now we have other problems to face. On the way down, did you see anything? A city?"

"No." There had been no time for that. All Dumarest

could remember was the world, the whine of atmosphere, the shocking advance of the ice, his own struggles with the controls; the final, sickening moment when the field had collapsed and they had fallen like a stone. "I saw nothing. And we don't even know which part of space this world could be in. The warp could have thrown us anywhere. Not that it matters. First, we have to survive."

"To escape this damned cold," agreed Arbush. He pounded gloved hands together. "Any ideas, Earl?"

"We must wait until dawn and then head towards the sun. Move south and hope to get out of this ice. For that we'll need food, ropes, and the means to make a fire. Ice axes too."

"What are they?"

"Things like picks with sharpened ends. Or one end sharp and one shaped like an axe. The *Styast* wouldn't have carried them; they'll have to be made."

"Tell me what you want and I'll make it," said Arbush. "I worked in metal once, years ago now, but some of the old skill remains. Anything else?"

"Pitons. Long spikes with eyes at the end to hold a rope. Hammers to bury them in the ice. More spikes to fit on our boots. Braided wire strong enough to carry seven times our combined weights. Packs in which to carry supplies." Dumarest rose. "We'd better get on with it."

The ship held all the material they needed. Dumarest stripped wire from the conduits while the minstrel busied himself with tools and a jury-rigged lastorch. Packs were fashioned from coverings stripped from the bunks, stiffened with fiber and sewn with wire. By the time they were finished, Arbush had made the ice axes. He held one out for inspection.

"These do, Earl?"

Rough blades had been welded to lengths of pipe, bound with cable at the ends to provide a grip. Dumarest hefted one, sent the point slamming into a scrap of metal.

"They'll do. Make a ring at the end so they can be carried on the wrist with a loop."

"I've made four." Arbush gestured towards them, then looked keenly at Dumarest. "You look bad. Those ribs hurting you?"

Drugs had eased the pain, but there could be internal bleeding which sapped his strength. Dumarest coughed, touched his lips, looked at a smear of blood on his hand.

"I'll be all right. You?"

"Bruised all to hell," said Arbush. "And my legs still seem numb. I got beaten up once and this feels the same. Well, I got over it then and I guess I'll get over it now." Pausing he added, quietly, "Do you think we've got a chance, Earl?"

"There's always a chance."

"Yes; and if there is, you'll take it. That's something else I read in your palm. Guts and luck both. I'm willing to ride with them." Arbush shivered. "Damn this cold! What we need is a drink. Maybe Beint had a secret bottle stashed somewhere."

He found it in a loop under the console; a metal flask of brandy disguised as a container of oil. After the first drink Dumarest replaced the cap.

"We'll need this later," he said. "Now let's get back to work."

At dawn they were ready; packs loaded, pitons heavy in pouches, coils of braided wire, hammers, axes hanging from roughly fashioned harnesses. Dumarest stood, thinking, mentally rechecking what they carried. A single item could mean their lives; once they had started, there would be no turning back.

Arbush came bustling from within the body of the wreck. He carried two lasers, and a bag which made small metallic clinkings.

"Here." He handed one of the guns to Dumarest. "A good thought, Earl. I'd forgotten."

"What's in the bag?"

"Money. Your ten thousand ermils." Arbush handed them over. "Some other things."

"Such as?" He watched as the minstrel tilted the bag. Rings showed, heavy bands set with precious gems, adornments wrenched from the fingers of the dead captain. A few octagonal coins, some others. The entire portable wealth of the *Styast*.

"There's no point in leaving it, Earl. A city can be as deadly as a jungle for a man who can't pay his way."

A hard-learned truth. Dumarest said, "Keep the rings and we'll split the money. Ready now?"

They climbed from the ship into a scintillating fairyland; the ice glowing with red and orange, green, blue, yellow, all the colors of the spectrum fired by the light of the sun. It was small, a blue-white orb which seared the vision, a compact patch of brightness in the sky. It hung low; against it they could only squint behind protectors of tinted plastic, goggles hastily improvised from the filters of broken scanners.

For a while they studied the terrain, grotesque figures muffled and shapeless; the minstrel's gilyre, miraculously preserved, hanging by a string from his pack.

"It's cold," said Arbush, gesturing towards the sun. "It looks hot, but it's cold. Radiating high in the ultra-violet and we must be a long way from it. The entire planet could be ice-bound, Earl."

A possibility, Dumarest had been on stranger worlds; but life existed in the most unexpected places. And if this planet held wealth of any kind it would have attracted exploiters; men who would build cities, visitors in ships.

If men were close. If the world was a habitated region. If the warp hadn't flung them into another space.

He said, "I'll take the lead. We'll be roped together. Keep back, but not too far. If I slip, dig in and take the strain."

"You've done this before," said Arbush. "Travelled over ice, I mean. How bad is it, Earl?"

Bad enough. Dumarest narrowed his eyes against the glare, catching deeper pools of color; shadows which revealed crevasses, mounds and distant peaks which would have to be climbed. Ahead rolled an undulating surface, scored and traced with gulleys of unknown depth; yet one which could be traversed without too much trouble during the day.

Relatively easy for men in good condition with proper equipment and clothing. Far from that, in their present condition.

"We'll head towards those peaks," he said, deciding. "Due south as far as I can gather. Aim for the pass between them. When we reach it, we'll take another sighting. Now, remember, keep the rope taut and stay alert."

There was no wind; for that he was grateful. No cloud and no flurry of frozen particles; but even so the going was hard. The surface was deceptive, perspective distorted, a multitude of snares hidden by the glare. Twice he stepped over the unseen edge of a crevasse, relying on the rope which jerked him to a halt and drew him back to safety. The third time a thin layer shattered beneath his boots and he fell further down than before, feeling the savage jerk at his harness as the life-line snapped taut.

Arbush's face was anxious as he drew him to safety.

"Your mouth, Earl, it's got blood on it. Do that again and you could shred your lungs. Why not let me take the lead?"

"You're too heavy." Dumarest wiped at the blood, already frozen. "If you slipped, I couldn't hold you. I'd follow you down." He looked at the sun. "We moved too soon. Later, if the sun rises higher, we can get a better view."

"Do we wait until then?"

"No. We can't be sure the sun will rise higher than it has. We'll just have to take more care."

He moved on, cautiously, testing every step of the way. The ice was crusted in places with frozen snow, patches which had hardened to hide what lay beneath. Like snails they crawled around them, crossing them only when there was no choice, anchoring the rope to axes driven deep as each man traversed the areas in turn.

Later the going improved; the ice which had been scored with cracks as if some mammoth hand had shattered the surface, growing more solid, less treacherous.

At noon they reached the pass and looked down into nightmare.

"We'll never be able to do it." Arbush, breathing heavily, slumped with his back against a hummock. The gilyre, swinging loose, rapped against the ice and made a soft, thrumming sound. "Earl, we'll have to find some other way. There has to be simpler route."

There probably was; finding it was something else. Dumarest looked at the sun; it was still low, even at the center of its swing. Lowering his eyes he took a sight; a jagged peak which rose like a rotten tooth, another beside it which seemed to bear a crenellated castle. From both summits smoke seemed to drift in thinning plumes, trapped snow carried by high-altitude winds.

Between where they sat and the distant peaks lay a mass of cracks and fissures, mounds, escarpments, gulleys, shimmering cliffs; the whole area torn and jagged as if a giant fork had stirred the surface. To reach it they would first have to descend a sheer wall which stretched as far as he could see on either side.

"We'll never do it," said Arbush again. "We've got to

drop five hundred feet and then cross that mess out there. Climbing, descending, up and down—and then what? More ice."

"We'll do it," said Dumarest. "We have to. Hold my legs while I take a look."

He eased forward as Arbush gripped his ankles, thrusting the upper part of his body over the edge. The ice was rough, cracked in places, ledged at spots on the way down. He studied them, impressing their position on his memory. Back up in his original position he said, "It won't be all that difficult. Pitons will hold the ropes and we can use the axes."

"Just like that?"

"There's no other way." Dumarest freed the coil of braided wire from his harness. "Join this to yours and make sure the knot is tight and smooth. It has to pass through the eyelet of a piton. We'll let ourselves down as far as we can go and then take it in stages."

At the edge Dumarest searched for a firm place and hammered one of the pitons in it, up to the eyelet. Through it he fed the joined rope, testing the knot with a jerk, making certain that it would slip through. Checking the end attached to his harness, he threw the remainder over the edge, then, gripping the length below the eyelet, slipped over the edge of the cliff.

A simple manoeuvre for a fit man, to let himself down a sheer drop while supporting his own weight on a trailing rope. But he wasn't fit, the braided wire was thin, cutting into his gloved palms, hard to grip; only the spikes on his boots enabled him to ease his way down towards a ledge he had spotted.

It lay a little towards the right, too far to reach; a narrow extension from the face, the edges frayed and weak. He dropped below it, kicked at the face and began to swing like the bob on a pendulum. Another kick, a third and his boots rasped on the ledge. Before he could swing away he slammed the point of an axe into the ice and hung on, breathing deeply.

"Earl! Are you all right?" Arbush's face was a blur, his voice a thin echo.

"Yes." Dumarest hammered home another piton. Through it he fed the free end of the rope, then released it from his harness. "Draw it up and do what I did. Hurry!"

It was easier for the minstrel; his weight taken up by the rope which Dumarest eased through the piton, the metal taking the strain. Gasping he clutched at holds, looking up then down, his mouth crusted with a rim of ice.

"Seventy feet," he said. "Maybe more. What do we do now?"

Dumarest pulled the rope, freeing it from above. "The same as before. And we do it as many times as we need to, until we reach the bottom."

"And if there are no ledges?"

"We'll use the axes to make holds, pitons to support our weight."

"And when they run out?"

"Then we start worrying." Dumarest handed the man the length of trailing rope. "Hang on to it. Help me take the strain."

They reached the bottom of the cliff as shadows thickened in the gullies, and the summits of the peaks flared with the dying light of the sun. Night caught them in the labyrinth and they found a narrow crevasse into which they huddled, as they ate rations warmed over a tiny fire.

"How long, Earl?" Arbush leaned forward a little as he sat, his face limned by the dying embers. "How far have we travelled today? Twenty miles? Ten? How long before we find a city?"

"As long as it takes."

"Until the food runs out. The fuel. Until one of us falls and kills himself. Until the cold gets us both. Well, no one promised that it would be easy." Arbush stirred, the gilyre falling from where he had placed it, to boom a little as it fell. "And, at least we can have a song."

It was a plaintive thing; a hopeless yearning carried on the pulse of strings, the whisper of ghost-drums born beneath the tapping of gloved fingers, the notes blurred and fuzzed yet skillfully blended. It faded to rise in a sudden crescendo; hard, brittle, this time seeming to shout defiance, the organ-notes of the minstrel's voice rising to send echoes rolling across the ice. Voice and music ended abruptly on a thin keening, which seemed to hang suspended in the air.

"Goodnight, Earl."

"Goodnight."

It was a time for sleep and yet Dumarest found it impossible to rest. Overstrained muscles joined with older injuries, accentuating their aches so that he turned and twisted, dozing to wake and turning to doze again. Drugs would have brought oblivion, would have at least ended the discomfort; but they, like everything else, were in limited supply.

Later, when they were essential, they would be used.

But time need not be wasted.

Sitting upright, Dumarest leaned his back against the ice. Facing him Arbush was asleep, his face covered, his gross frame jerking as if he dreamed. One hand was lying in the long-dead embers of the fire, the other clutched his gilyre. Above the stars blazed with fading glory, their light diffused by a thin skein of cloud, a gossamer veil carried on an unseen wind. A wind which could lower, cloud which could thicken; a storm could fill the air with a raging blizzard.

If so, they were as good as dead.

Was this where it was all going to end? The long search over. The path he had followed since a boy; the hard, bitter, blood-stained path among the scattered worlds to end here on this unknown planet, beneath a nameless sun?

The stars seemed to swirl, to take on other configurations, to become a mane of silver hair. Derai whom he had known, who had promised so much, who had left him to dream in endless, subjective sleep. As others had left him; too many others. Kalin, Lallia, Mayenne—all now dead. Dust and fragments of the past.

The wind gusted lower, sighing, holding the wail of a Ghenka song. The metal plate on which they had built the fire rasped over the ice as he fell against it. Sleep finally came with a host of memories, faces which loomed close to fall away, to be replaced by others distorted in the fabric of nightmare.

He woke with a hand clamped hard over his mouth, his nose.

"Earl!" Arbush's voice was a strained whisper. "Earl! Wake up! There's something watching us!"

Chapter Seven

It was past dawn, the sky a blanket of nacreous cloud, the sun a glowing patch of milky brightness. The cloud had robbed the ice of color; now it stretched in a mass of tormented white and grey, blurring as it met the cloud so that it was hard to see the horizon.

Dumarest said, "Where?"

"Over there." Arbush pointed to where a ridge stood, about a hundred yards to the east of the crevasse in which they had slept. "I woke and it was light. You seemed to be resting, so I thought I'd light a fire and warm some food before waking you. I'd stood up to stretch and I turned and saw it."

"Saw what?"

"I don't know. It was white, roundish, about as tall as a man, maybe a little taller. It moved, which was what caught my eye; had it remained still it would have been invisible."

Whatever it had been, it wasn't visible now. Which meant nothing. The area was laced with fissures, mounds to provide cover, a thousand places in which to hide. Even now, it could be moving closer. If so the blind-end, shallow crevasse in which they stood could turn into a trap.

Dumarest said, "We'd better get moving."

"Now? Without anything to eat?"

"We'll stop later. If something's watching us it may follow. If it does, we could spot it. You only saw the one?"

"Yes."

"And you're sure it was something which moved?"

"I'm sure." Arbush was defensive. "I know what you're thinking, Earl. A man freshly awake, turning; seeing a patch of moving shadow and mistaking it for something else. But it was there and it was real enough. If I'd been holding the laser I'd have taken a shot at it."

The blind, thoughtless reaction of a man faced with the unknown.

Dumarest turned, wincing as he headed towards the mouth of the crevasse. The sleep had done little good and the drugs he had taken earlier had lost their effect. Now his body was a mass of pain, the taste of blood raw in his throat, hands and legs numbed by the cold. He stamped, beating his hands to restore the circulation. Arbush watched as he fumbled for ampoules and the hypogun from his pack.

"Let me do that, Earl." His gloved hands were clumsy and he cursed as the tiny vials fell to the ice. Stripping off the coverings, he thrust his bare hands beneath his clothing, holding them close to his loins. Warmed the fingers were more flexible and he loaded the instrument, firing it as his hands turned blue.

Dumarest caught the hypogun as it fell.

"How about yourself?"

"I ache," admitted the minstrel. "That beam must have damaged my kidneys." He blinked as Dumarest fired pain-killers into his blood. "I thought you wanted to conserve that stuff?"

"I did," said Dumarest. "Until we needed it. That is now."

"Because of what I saw?" Arbush frowned, thinking. "It looked like a man," he said slowly. "But if it had been a man, surely he would have come closer? Joined us. A beast then, but here, in this wilderness?"

It was possible, a wanderer from some other region, a creature obeying instinctive promptings. Scenting food, perhaps; attracted by the fire, the music, the song. If so, and if it came close enough to be killed, it would be an asset. The meat for food, the bones for fuel, the stomach a container in which to boil a stew.

Unless it reached them first in which case it, not they, would eat.

Laser in hand Dumarest led the way from the crevasse, climbing up to the far edge, taking a sight on the peak which rose like a rotten tooth and heading towards it; his eyes moving from side to side, every sense alert.

The caution slowed them down. Each crack had to be checked, every mound carefully circumnavigated. Behind him Arbush glanced constantly over his shoulder, several times stumbling to fall, jerking at the rope which joined them.

At noon they stopped to eat; firing scraps of fuel with a laser, warming cans of meat, a measure of basic, following it with a gulp of brandy.

Dumarest had chosen a sheltered spot against a crusted hummock; a shallow indentation providing some protection against the wind which now gusted with irregular force. A chance which had to be taken: but the hummock was high, the sides sleek, the area before them relatively flat and affording good visibility.

The meal finished he opened three cans of meat and tipped out the contents, to lie in a small heap next to the dead ashes of the fire.

"Bait," said Arbush, understanding. "Are you going to kill it, Earl?"

"Maybe, but first I want to see what it is."

"An animal, following us; what else is there to know?"

What it was, what it fed on, whether or not it was alone. Answers which Dumarest kept to himself. He said, "We'll back away from the hummock. You look left, I'll look right. If anything's waiting out there, don't fire until you have to."

Nothing was waiting. Well away from where he had placed the food Dumarest found a mound and dropped behind it, looking back the way they had come. Minutes passed, the wind blowing, carrying a wisp of snow; frozen particles which stung the exposed areas of his face. Beside him Arbush moved restlessly, lacking the trained patience of a hunter; the stolid indifference to hardship which Dumarest had learned when barely old enough to walk.

And, finally, they came.

Arbush sucked in his breath. "God, Earl they're—"

"Be quiet!"

Dumarest had seen them before the other: roundish shapes, dingily white, moving to freeze into invisibility before moving again. Five of them, which could have been animals shaped something like bears.

But animals would never have moved with such calculated deliberation, would never have merged to break into positions of advantage; to have stood watch while some of their number scooped up the discarded food, to place it in what could only be pouches.

"Men!" breathed Arbush. "Earl! They're men!"

Dumarest caught him as he was about to rise, to shout and reveal their position.

"Keep down! Keep quiet!"

"But—"

"They're men," agreed Dumarest. "But what kind? Scavengers? Thieves? Cannibals?"

In this frozen hell anything was possible, and there were many cultures which regarded a stranger as a source of food. Conveniently packaged protein—the need to survive made its own rules.

"They must have seen us crash," whispered Arbush. "Stumbled upon us while they were searching for the ship. But they must have a place to live, Earl. Caves, maybe, anything. We've got money and could bribe them to help us, to guide us to a city."

His yearning was an echo in his tones. Dumarest heard it, recognised it; yet recognised too the danger Arbush had overlooked. A bargain needed two to make it; what was to stop the strangers from taking all they owned and giving nothing in return?

Yet, without them, what chance did they have to survive?

Dumarest said, "This is what we'll do. You stand and wave. Don't move; wait for them to come towards you. When they are fairly close, step out to confront them. I'll cover you. If they make any attempt to attack we'll shoot them down."

"Kill them, Earl?"

"Kill all but one. We'll need information." Harshly he added, "And we could use their clothes."

Crouched on the ice, hands extended, hands tight around the laser, finger clamped on the trigger, Dumarest stared over the barrel at the distant shapes. Beside him Arbush rose, shouting, waving.

"Hi, there! I'm here! Over here!"

The little group froze, then scattered; running, dispersing, blending into the ice. For long minutes there was nothing and then they reappeared, closer now, tiny plumes of vapor streaming from their muffling cowls.

Again Arbush shouted. "Please help me. I need help. My friend is badly hurt."

Not a lie, and they would know that he wasn't alone. Dumarest fought the desire to cough, feeling the warm liquid in his throat, the taste of blood in his mouth. He felt a growing lassitude, the edges of his vision becoming rimmed with black. He had lain immobile for too long. Internal blood-loss and the cold was taking its effect; the hypothermia could be as fatal as a knife in the heart.

Determinedly he blinked, shaking his head, narrowing his eyes as he stared over the barrel of the laser at the advancing group. They were cautious, as wary as beasts as they approached; looking to either side and up towards the sky.

Up?

He turned as the group dissolved, racing back and away; he saw the nacreous glare of the sky, the man-like things silhouetted against it, one of which was diving like an arrow towards where he lay.

"Earl!" Arbush yelled as Dumarest rolled, slamming the weight of his body against the minstrel's legs, knocking him down and to one side, to sprawl against the ice. "Earl, what—"

Steam exploded from where he had stood, a gushing spout of scalding water mixed with fragments of shattered ice; the heat and noise of the explosion added to the concussion of the shock-wave.

Vapor wreathed them, settled, froze in a disguising blanket of frost. Through it Dumarest saw the thing which had attacked them and its two companions pass on; more explosions rising above the ice from the missiles they fired as, wheeling, they turned to vanish into the sky towards the south.

"Armoured men," said Arbush wonderingly. "Fitted with flying packs and carrying guns. A hunting party Earl? Mistaking us for those others we saw? But they were men. Who would hunt down men from the sky?"

"I don't know." Dumarest rose, conscious of his fatigue, his weakness. "But they've stopped our chances of getting help from those we saw. They must think we lured them into a snare."

"Some could be dead," said Arbush. "Shall we look?"

"No. There could be others. The way they must be feeling, they'll kill us on sight and I wouldn't blame them." Dumarest looked toward the south. "Those flyers were dropping, maybe heading towards a landing place. There must be a city there, somewhere. A camp at least. We have to find it."

"And soon." Arbush began to shiver, his face blotched, unhealthy; the tip of his nose deathly white. Frostbite which would spread to his toes, his hands. "Earl, it will have to be soon."

Adara said, patiently, "Eloise, why be so stubborn? Why can't you be reasonable?"

"Which means what?" she flared. "Be reasonable—do it my way. At times, Adara, you make me sick!"

"That isn't fair!"

"But true. You saw the ship. You said yourself that it would land close, and what have you done about it? Nothing. What has anyone else done? The same. Well, I've waited long enough."

Too long, she thought. Years too long; but up until now there had been no chance, and she'd had no choice but to wait. Now things were different. A ship had landed and it was close—and no one seemed to care!

"Eloise!" He stepped towards her, his hands rising to grip her shoulders; the action betraying his concern, his need. "You can't go out there, you know that. Even if you could, what do you hope to find? Don't you remember how it was before? You were lucky then. It was only by an accident that you were found. I—"

"You had guts then," she said coldly. "You saw what happened and did something about it. Well, now it's my turn."

Defeated, he let his hands fall from her furred shoulders. She was wearing thick garments of synthetic material, a cap of fur on her head, thick boots on her legs. Outdoor garb for those who chose to indulge in long walks outside the city. Beyond the transparent doors of the vestibule in which they stood, he could see others similarly dressed. Not many, for few chose to expose themselves to the rigors of the cold; but enough to make touches of color against the starkness of the ringing hills, the paths crisp with frost.

He said, "You don't even know which way to go. You don't know how far. It will be dark before you reach the hills, and then what? You couldn't go on even if the Monitors would let you."

"But you—"

"That was different. You were close—and I had permission."

"Of course." She was acid. "You would have had to have that."

"Naturally." He was unaffected by her gibe, not recognizing the insult. "How else to gain the aid of the Monitors? You don't think for a moment you could scale the hills alone, do you? Eloise why can't you be willing to—"

"Be reasonable?"

"—face the facts. At least check with Camolsaer."

The obvious which she had forgotten or, if not forgotten, had not yet done; perhaps reluctant to face the truth. She looked at Adara with sudden suspicion. He, knowing of her interest, must have already checked. Why hadn't he told her what he had learned? And then, looking into his face, his eyes, she guessed the answer. He, least of all, would want to be the bringer of bad news.

With abrupt decision she walked to the nearest terminal.

"Eloise. What news about the ship?"

"Which ship?"

"The one which crashed." With an effort she mastered her impatience; with Camolsaer it was essential to be precise. "Two days ago, at evening, an object which could have been a vessel crossed the sky close to Instone. It seemed to be in trouble. Did it land?"

"An impact was noted."

"Where?"

"At a point about fifty miles to the north and east. The exact location is—"

"Never mind." The figures would mean nothing to her. "Tell me what was found."

"No investigation has been made."

"What? A ship crashed and you didn't even make an investigation?"

"The object could have been a vessel in distress, or it could not. No signals were received, therefore the conclusion is that it was not a vessel. In any case, it is not within the boundaries of Instone."

"Just like that," she said bitterly. "It doesn't fall into your nice, neat pattern and so it doesn't concern you. What about the crew?"

"If the object was not a vessel there would have been no crew."

The thing was playing with her, she was certain of it. Nothing could be that stupid. Furiously she glared at the facing of the terminal, the plate beneath her hand, the scanners which looked too much like eyes. Blank, empty eyes in a blank, emotionless face. The visage of a Monitor. A machine.

Tightly she said, "Assume that the object noted *was* a vessel in distress. Assume that it carried a crew, that it crashed, that it was unable to radio for help. What would be the chances of survival?"

"For the crew, none."

"Elucidate."

"The impact noted was of a high order of magnitude. The chance that any living thing survived is remote. If they had, the hostile environment would have precluded extended survival. Also, there have been signs of Krim activity. Monitor patrols have dispersed several groups and destroyed several individuals. If nothing else, they would have terminated the existence of any who may have survived the crash."

And there it was, she thought bleakly. The answer which Adara had been reluctant to give. All neatly wrapped up, tied with a red ribbon and dropped on her plate like an unwelcome gift. One he could accept, but she could not.

As she turned from the terminal he said, "You see, Eloise? There is no hope."

"Because Camolsaer says so?" She stared at him, skin, bone, flesh and blood; something on which to vent her anger, the rage born of frustration, of disappointment. "It could be wrong."

"No! Camolsaer is never wrong!"

"How can you be sure? It has taken a handful of data and from it drawn a conclusion. Something, it could have been a ship, landed hard on the ice. Therefore, nothing in it could have lived. Therefore, if anything had lived, the cold would kill it. Therefore, if it had lived and the cold didn't kill it, the Krim would. Is that what you call being right?"

"Facts, Eloise."

"We don't know the facts," she stormed. "Why haven't Monitors gone to investigate? All right, so it's beyond the city; but men could be out there, still living, waiting, hoping, fighting to stay alive."

"If so, they will find us."

"More logic?" She was wasting her time and knew it.

Neither Adara, nor any of them, would think of doubting Camolsaer. God had spoken—so let it be. A comforting, safe and convenient philosophy. Flatly she said, "I spoke of men, Adara. I don't think you know what a man is. I don't think anyone here does. Men don't give up. They fight to the last. Injuries, cold, enemies; they face and beat them all. If they didn't they wouldn't be men."

"Supermen, surely?"

"Men!" she said savagely. "Dear God—send me a man!"

"Eloise!"

She turned from him, ignoring his hurt, the bruised look in his eyes. Once a woman had warned her against doing what she had just done. Never to throw doubt on a man's masculinity. Never to demean him, to hurt his pride. Her face had carried scars to emphasize the lesson.

"Eloise!"

"Leave me for now, Adara. Please."

Later, perhaps, she would make amends; but now, alone, she stepped towards the doors, the cold air outside, the scatter of people, the tall figures of Monitors shining in the fading light.

Soon it would be dark. Another night of cold and wind, the stars hidden by clouds, the air heavy with the threat of snow; a blizzard which would sweep across the ice. Camolsaer had been right. Nothing human could live in such conditions. She had been a fool to hope.

Chapter Eight

~~~~~~~~~~~~~~~~~~~~~~~~~~~~~~~~~~~~

The cave was little more than a shallow fissure in a wall of ice, the sides closing to meet above, the walls and floor rough with jagged projections. A small space into which they could barely squeeze, could only crouch. But it had saved their lives.

The cave and the wind which carried the snow away from the opening; the blinding mass of whiteness filled the air, accentuating the darkness of the night. The wind which caught at the crude wick thrust into a can of nutrient paste and sent shadows dancing from the guttering flame.

Dumarest shielded it with his hands.

Facing him Arbush stirred, wincing, forcing himself to stay awake. His face was blotched with white patches, feet and hands devoid of feeling. Ice rimmed the edge of his hood and his eyes were bloodshot.

"Tomorrow, Earl," he said. "You're sure?"

"You saw what I did."

"Which was nothing. A column of air which quivered towards the south."

"Rising air," said Dumarest. "Warm air. It has to be the city."

The haven for which they had searched for how long? Too long; longer and they would both be dead. The food was gone, the fuel; the drugs remained, only enough to kill their pain for a final effort. Looking at the minstrel Dumarest knew that he saw a depiction of himself; face drawn, frostbitten, the eyes bloodshot, raw with squinting against the wind, the glare of the ice. But, if anything, he looked worse; the dried blood on his chin caked and dried, replenished when he coughed.

Blood from torn and ruptured lungs. Only the drugs enabled him to keep going. Drugs and the will to survive.

A scrap of metal rested between them, the plate on which they had built their fires while the fuel had lasted. Next to it lay one of the lasers. Dumarest picked it up, aimed it at the metal and triggered the weapon. A small patch glowed red, another, half a dozen more; the transmuted energy of the weapon giving a faint semblance of comfort.

"Don't use all the charge," warned Arbush. "We might need it later."

"We still have the other gun."

"Of course. You would think of that. You've thought of everything. If it hadn't been for you—" Arbush broke off, shaking his head. "How about the rest of that brandy?"

He needed it, they both did; fuel to give them energy. To save it for later would be to save it too long. Arbush shared it, looking into the empty can which served as a container, the five ounces of spirit it contained.

"Odd, Earl, how at times like this you remember things. I took my first drink when I was twelve. It was at the festival and I sneaked a cup of wine. There was a girl, I thought she was an angel, but it must have been the wine. Twelve," he said broodingly. "A long time ago now. Too long."

Dumarest sipped at his brandy, nursing it, savoring it as it trickled down his throat. With care, it would last until dawn.

"What made you start playing?"

"That?" Arbush glanced at the gilyre, now coated with ice, the strings crusted with snow. "I don't know, really. There was a minstrel at our village, a transient, and he took a shine to me. I followed him when he left and he taught me to play. I was good at it, even then, and there were advantages. A good tune, a song, and the girls fell into my arms. I was young then, of course, not so fat as I am now; but it wouldn't have mattered. Sometimes, even now—" He shook his head, sighing. "Well, all that's in the past."

"And the *Styast?*" Dumarest wasn't really interested but they had to stay awake. To fall silent would be to yield to the fumes of the brandy, the lethargy which would bring the sleep preceding death. "How did you tie up with Eglantine?"

"That pig!" Arbush made a spitting sound. "A mistake, Earl. I rode on one ship too many and found I was trapped. Debts which couldn't be paid and a rut into which I fell. The wrong part of space for a minstrel to earn a living, even if he is young and good to look at. I am neither." Shrewdly he added, "As a traveler you should know the danger of taking passage on the wrong ship, of landing in the wrong world."

Planets without industry, backward worlds on which it was impossible to earn the price of a passage out; places on which the unwary could be stranded, often to starve to death. Handlers with warped minds who withheld the numbing drugs, and watched as those who had travelled Low screamed their lungs raw with the agony of resurrection. Small-minded, frustrated men trapped in the metal shells they rode between the stars, envious of those with wider horizons.

"Yes," said Dumarest bleakly. "I know."

"What makes a man do it?" mused Arbush softly. "To leave home and family and push into the unknown. I had friends, prospects; yet I left them all to follow a man who could make music with the touch of his fingers. Had I stayed there would have been wealth, girls to enjoy, ease and comfort to the end of my days. I must have been mad. All of us who drift like dust between the stars, all must be mad."

Beyond the mouth of the cave the wind gusted, sighing as if in agreement; the crude candle guttering, shadows casting thick patches on the minstrel's face, making him look suddenly old.

"Perhaps we are looking for something," said Dumarest.

"Perhaps." Arbush nodded his agreement. "Wealth, adventure, the love of women—who can tell? I wanted all those things and more. Fame, renown, the galaxy at my feet. Instead I found toil and tribulation, a stinking berth in a rotting ship. And you, Earl? What are you seeking?"

"A planet. A world called Earth."

"Earth?" Arbush sipped at his brandy. "Surely you are joking. Earth is a legend."

"No."

"But—"

"It is real," said Dumarest flatly. "It exists. I know. I was born there."

To run half-naked and half-starved, to catch his food

with the aid of a sling, a thrown stone, a knife; small beasts which lurked among rocks which he had to catch or starve. A hard, bitter time in which hunger ruled, in which gentleness had taken no part.

He sipped at his brandy.

"Tell me about it," said Arbush quietly. "If we live, it could supply the material for a song."

"An old world," said Dumarest. "The surface scarred and torn by ancient wars. There is a great silver moon and the skies are blue when not fleeced with cloud. The sun is yellow, the seas a dark green when not grey. I left it as a boy, stowing away on a ship. The captain was more kind than I deserved. He should have evicted me; instead, he let me work my passage. I have been traveling ever since."

"But if you left it, Earl, you must know where it is. Surely you could take passage on a ship going that way?"

"Which way?" Dumarest was curt. "I told you that I was young and, perhaps filled with that madness you spoke of. The past was behind me, I wanted only to look ahead. For a while I rode with the captain and then he died, and I was on my own."

A bad time in which he had learned the hard way; work at anything which came to hand, fighting in the rings when there was no work, taking cuts the scars of which he would always carry, killing when he'd had no choice. And moving, always moving, travelling from world to world; ever deeper into the galaxy, towards the center where the suns were close and planets thick. Into a region where the very name of Earth was a legend, its position unknown.

"No almanac lists the coordinates," he said. "No navigational chart shows any world by that name. You, everyone, thinks it is only a world of legend. Yet I know that it is real and, being real, it is to be found. One day I shall find it."

With the aid of clues picked up over the years; fragments of data which could, eventually, be assembled into a whole. A second name, Terra; the sun around which it circled, a G-type star; the names given to constellations seen from its northern hemisphere; the sector of space in which it must lie.

He said again, "One day I will find it."

Arbush sipped at his brandy then said, quietly, "Yes, Earl. I think that you will."

Dawn broke with clear skies, the storm over; the snow which had been carried on the wind now lying in a soft blanket of deceptive smoothness through which they floundered, fighting every inch of the way.

With snow-shoes it would have been simple, progress fast and relatively undemanding; but they had no snow-shoes and nothing from which they could be made. Blue, shivering, Arbush collapsed to roll and stare blankly at the sky.

"Earl, I'm not going to make it. Maybe you'd better press on alone."

"No."

"I'm beat. My hands are frozen, my feet. I've lost all feeling in my fingers." He tried to smile, a death-like grimace which cracked the rim of ice on his lips. "What good's a minstrel who can't pluck a string? Leave me, Earl; but, before you go—"

"I'll kill you when I have to, not before." Dumarest was harsh. "Get up, you fat fool!"

"I can't!"

"You can! You will!"

Arbush closed his eyes, his head lolling from side to side, too exhausted to argue.

Dumarest stared down at him, fighting the dizziness which made snow and sky wheel in nauseating circles; the weakness of legs and body which threatened to send him to the ground. It was tempting to rest for a while; to sit and lie and cease all effort. To close his eyes and yield to the fatigue which dulled his brain. To sleep never to waken. To find the endless, eternal peace of death.

"You've got to help me. I'm in pain. I need your help to use the rest of the drugs."

It was like talking to the dead.

"Get up on your feet, man. I can't make it alone. I need your help. Get up, damn you. You owe it to me."

Arbush whispered, "Sorry, Earl. Sorry. I—"

"Talk," sneered Dumarest. "The madness you spoke about. You wanted adventure, you said. Or did you take a woman who wasn't yours and had to run? Was that your courage? No wonder you stayed on the *Styast*. Who else would have you? A fat, lying, dirty coward, full of bad music and pitiful songs. You should have died when we landed. Shalout would have had more guts than you. Even Beint, with only one hand, would have put up a better fight. You scum! You filth! Get up and act like a man!"

Anger was a good anodyne for despair, but the attempt to arouse it met with the same result as the appeal.

Only the spur of physical pain was left.

Dumarest knelt, gasping, feeling the blood in his throat and his mouth. He coughed and spat a ruby stream, dark, filled with bubbles. Resting his fingers on the cold flesh of the minstrel's face, he pressed the tips against the closed eyes. Gently, too much would blind, not enough have no effect.

Arbush moaned, writhing, one arm lifting to weakly knock the hand aside.

Dumarest coughed again and beat his hands together, steadily, relentlessly; feeling the numbed flesh begin to tingle. Warmed he sent his right hand over the fat body, feeling the swell of the rotund belly, the thickness of the thighs, the tender flesh between.

Gripping, he squeezed.

Arbush screamed like a stricken beast.

"Earl! For God's sake!"

"Up!" snarled Dumarest. "Get on your feet!"

He fumbled for the last of the drugs as the minstrel heaved himself from the snow, used them, threw the hypogun to one side.

Pointing to a ridge which cut the sky ahead he said, "There. We must reach it before we stop. Now move!"

They made the ridge, another beyond it, a third over which they heaved themselves to rest; gasping, looking back over their trail. It wound like the path of a drunken snake; twice the length necessary had they been fit, able to surmount the mounds and hummocks around which it wended. Something moved at the far end.

"They're after us," wheezed Arbush. "Those men we saw before. Following us and waiting until we drop."

Scavengers, or simply men wanting revenge for those killed by the flying, armoured figures. Dumarest looked at the sky; as yet it was clear, but should the flyers come they would present easy targets.

He said, "Let's get moving. The city should lie beyond that rim."

"We could signal, maybe," panted Arbush as he beat

his way through the snow. "Use the lasers, tie something on an axe to use as a flag, anything."

"Maybe."

"Why not, Earl? They could come out and get us. Damn it, we need some help."

Food, warmth, medical attention, all could be waiting. A spur which kept Arbush moving, arms and legs working as if parts of a machine, his mind lost in an enticing dream.

"Steam baths," he whispered. "Hot showers. Oils applied by lovely girls. Meats, hot, with crisp skins and filled with succulent juices. Mulled wine, spiced so as to tingle the tongue; fires, ovens, heat to take the chill from flesh and bone. Once I was on a hot world, Sere; a place of jungle and desert, the sun like a furnace in the sky. I hated it then, but I would give half of what remains of my life to be there now."

His voice broke, took on the thin, keening of a song; a dirge which held the wail of distraught women, the cry of a bereft child.

It ended when they saw the city.

"Earl!" Arbush turned, snapped from his delirium; his mottled face was haggard, defeated. "How the hell are we going to reach it?"

It lay in the cup of a valley, a gem held in an upturned palm; towers, spires and rounded domes, the flat expanse of walls, the spread of terraces covered with transparent material which glowed in the sun.

A paradise in the wilderness, enchanted, enticing— unobtainable.

Crouched on the rim Dumarest studied it, fighting the blurring of his eyes; the wavering of planes and lines which, at times, gave the impression of looking through water.

It could almost have been a mirage.

Almost, but no mirage he had ever seen had rested in the cup of a valley; and the flyers he had seen had been real enough. No mirage had fired the missile which had almost killed him. And those flyers must have come from this city.

He studied it, ignoring Arbush's babble; the low mutter of his voice as, once again, he yielded to the fogs which misted his brain. Around the place lay a broad circle of flat ground now covered with a dust of snow; more snow heaped in high dunes at the half-mile expanse of smooth terrain. Once reached, it would be easy to cross.

Reaching it was something else.

The valley was deep; the rim on which he crouched a quarter mile above the heaped snow at its foot. A smooth, sheer drop, as if something had cut away the rock and ice in a mathematical pattern. A bowl, wider at the rim than at the foot, the surface roughly concave; the curve flattening as it descended.

To either side it was the same.

Blinking he withdrew from the edge, gripped the minstrel's shoulder, shook him, sent the flat of his gloved hand across the mottled cheek.

"We're here," he snapped. "We've arrived. All we have to do is to climb down a slope."

"All?" Arbush sucked in his breath, his eyes bloodshot, but clear. "I was dreaming, Earl. I thought I had wings. We need wings. How else are we to get down?"

"The same way as we did before. Pitons and ropes. We'll take it in short, easy stages."

Stages which had to be short, but which would never be easy. Before it had been hard, now it would be almost impossible.

Dumarest fumbled at his pack, his pouches. Four pitons, two axes, rope and a hammer. Arbush had the same, aside from the pitons of which he had six.

Ten pitons, eighty feet at a time, but the drops would be too long and still they would not have reached the bottom. He looked at the axes, the rings at their ends. They would help, but it still wasn't enough. Back at the rim he searched the lower expanse. The wall, appearing smooth, was not. A thin fissure ran in a diagonal, from a point a hundred feet down to another twice as far. And they had the lasers, one charged, the other almost exhausted.

"We'll start from here. Two pitons buried deep. Feed the rope through one and bind it on the other, so it will take the strain as you let me down. When it reaches the middle, lash it tight. I'll make a hold and signal. When I do, feed through the rest of the rope, knock free the extra piton and follow me down as you did before."

"Earl—"

"There's a fissure down there in which we can rest." Dumarest picked up one of the hammers. "Let's get at it."

It was too hard, his body too weak. Before he had

struck a half-dozen blows, he knew it was impossible. Dropping the hammer he drew the near-depleted laser, aimed it, sent the beam to melt a hole into which he rammed the piton. Three blows and it was secure. The other quickly followed.

Quickly, because there was no time to dwell on the difficulty of the task. No time to allow the final surge of energy to subside.

Two stages and they reached the fissure to lie gasping, to crawl down its length; to face again the impossible task of crawling like flies down a wall of ice.

Dumarest threw aside the exhausted laser, used the other, finished the job with blows of the hammer; each stroke sent waves of nausea through his mind, filling his vision with darts of color.

On the third stage down, he knew they would never make it.

He hung on the end of the rope, Arbush above lashed to a piton; a bulky figure like a grotesque spider caught in a frayed web. His voice was thin, strained, "Earl!"

Dumarest moved, looking upwards, the turn of his head taking an age, the effort to shift mountains.

"Earl! God, man, the rope!"

It was stretching, overstrained; the cold making metal and plastic brittle, wires yielding within their sheaths. Old material, bought cheap, made to last long beyond its time. Breaking even as he watched.

Looking down he saw the mounded drift of snow, the outcurve of the wall. Falling he would hit it, be thrown from it, to plummet well away from its foot. Away from the snow, the only thing which could break his fall.

"Earl!"

He jerked, dropped, hovered for a moment and then dropped again, strands breaking, others stretching to break in turn; the entire rope giving with a suddenness which sent him falling.

Falling to the wall, the ground, the frozen hardness which would pulp his flesh and shatter his bones.

Chapter Nine

There were small sounds, clickings; and for a moment he thought he was back in the *Styast,* strapped to the control chair, reliving a segment of the past. Then he felt deft touches, the pull of gentle suction, something eased from around his temples.

"All right," said a voice. "You can open your eyes now."

Dumarest looked at a fog of nacreous brightness, a mist in which objects took shape and substance; solidifying into a ceiling, lights, oddly shaped machines, the face of a man.

"I am Dras. What is your name?" He smiled at the response. "Good. As Camolsaer predicted, you have recovered with total awareness of personal identity."

"Camolsaer?"

"You can sit up now." Dras ignored the question. "That's right. If you feel a little nausea it will pass. Now just relax, while I make a few extra tests."

He was sitting on a long, wide couch covered with a dull green material, placed close to a machine which sprouted suction-tipped wires. A diagnostic machine which must have been monitoring his condition. As the man bustled around him, instruments making soft impacts on his skin, Dumarest examined his body.

He was nude, wasted, muscles clearly ridged against the bone. The thin lines of old scars showed on his torso, together with others more recently made.

"You were in a bad way when the Monitors brought you in," said the man as he checked his findings. "Extensive frostbite, several ribs broken, your lungs terribly lacerated. There was also a high degree of debilitation, together with large areas of bruising and multiple points of internal hemorrhage." He added, casually, "You were also in a state of terminal shock."

"My companion?"

"Is well. His injuries were not as extensive as yours. He was released a month ago."

A month? Dumarest looked again at his body. A long passage travelling Low would have produced a similar result; body-fat used to maintain life, tissue wasted, muscles beginning to shrink.

He said, "How long have I been here?"

"A long time. First, we had to put you into an amniotic tank and by-pass your normal organic functions with a life support apparatus. The lungs, of course, had to be regrown from available tissue. Later, after the grafting, electrical stimulation was applied to maintain the efficiency of the muscles. Healing was completed with the use of slow-time."

"How long?"

"A month, subjective. You were kept unconscious by direct electrical stimulation of the sleep center of the brain." Dras gestured to where a thin band of metal, fitted with inner pads and electrodes, stood beside the couch on an instrument table. "Camolsaer decided that longer would be inadvisable."

Camolsaer had been right. Slow-time accelerated the metabolism, as quick-time slowed it. The body lived faster than normal—the danger was that energy was used faster than it could be replaced, even with the aid of intravenous feeding. No wonder he was wasted.

Dras said, eagerly, "Are you interested in medical matters? If so, I have full charts and details of your original condition, together with the treatment followed and steps taken. Camolsaer, naturally, directed the pattern to be followed; but, I must admit, I found it most stimulating."

A doctor starved of customers; a frustrated surgeon who had relished the opportunity to test his skill. Dumarest swung his legs over the edge of the couch.

"Am I free to go now?"

"Yes," said Dras reluctantly. "I would like your later cooperation in conducting a series of tests of my own, but that is up to you."

"My clothes?"

They were in a cabinet; pants, boots and tunic all bright and smooth, the material refurbished. Even the knife had been polished and honed. One of the pockets was heavy with the weight of coins.

"Your companion selected them from among those you wore," explained Dras. "The knife, I understand, is a symbol of rank. The laser, of course, could not be allowed."

"By whom?"

"Camolsaer." Dras sounded surprised at the question, a man who, having breathed all his life, should suddenly be asked why he breathed. A mystery, one to be added to the rest; but if the minstrel had been released a month ago he could have the answers.

"Arbush," said Dumarest. "My companion. Where can I find him?"

"A moment." Dras crossed to where a machine protruded from a wall. A ledge three feet above the floor, a metal plate above it, a grill; lenses glowed as he rested his hand on the ledge. "Dras. Where is Arbush?"

The answer came immediately, the voice flat as it droned from the grill.

"Corridor 137. Point 37."

"Outside," said Dras turning. "He's waiting outside."

Arbush had changed, fat dissolved from his body to reveal the firm outline of bone, the bulk of muscle; but he was still big, still round.

"Earl!" His hand lifted, extended, the fingers touching, gripping a shoulder. "Man, it's good to see you!"

Dumarest returned the gesture. "You're looking well."

"Better than the last time you saw me, eh?" Arbush smiled. He was wearing a coverall of dull brown, the sleeves flecked with minute patches of yellow as if some thick liquid had splashed and dried. "I was as near dead as I ever want to be. When the rope broke and you fell and I—" He broke off, shuddering. "A bad time, Earl."

Lashed to a piton, hanging helplessly from a rod thrust into a sheer wall; without a rope, a companion, any means of escape. Left to swing, to wait, to freeze and die. To envy, perhaps, the one who had fallen.

Dumarest said, "What happened?"

"A miracle. They must have seen us from the city. Camolsaer sent out Monitors and one arrived, just in time to catch you as you fell. It wasn't gentle; there wasn't time for that. It just grabbed you and I guess it must have knocked you out. At least you hung limp as it carried you away. Then two others came for me."

"Monitors?"

"Those things like armoured men that we saw flying. One of them shot at us. They aren't men, Earl. And they don't usually fly. They wear attachments for that."

"And Camolsaer?"

"They didn't tell you?" Arbush shrugged. "Well, they didn't tell me either. I guess they're so used to it that they take it for granted. Like having to explain gravitation; no one ever does, you just know it's there. Camolsaer runs the city."

"A man?"

"No, a machine. At least I guess it is. I've never seen it." Arbush glanced along the corridor. "Tell you what, let's get something to drink. Good stuff, Earl; as fine a wine as I've tasted anywhere. And you don't have to pay for it."

Dumarest said, dryly, "That's convenient."

"You don't have to pay for anything. Think of it, Earl. Clothes, food, wine, entertainment, all free. Every damned thing you want, you can get by asking for it. Just by asking. I've got a better room than you could get in any top-class hotel. Clothes which would cost a fortune, on any planet. All the things I dreamt about on the ice; hot baths, succulent meats, everything, all on tap."

"Including those willing, wanton girls?"

"Those too." Arbush was bland. "There's one in particular who is very interested in you, Earl. She's bent my ear for hours on end, wanting to know about the warp, the ship, how you managed to keep us alive." He sobered a little. "Earl, out there on the ice, you said some pretty hard things. Did them too."

"So?"

"I just wanted to let you know I don't hold it against you. It had to be done. At the time I felt like murder; but, well, let's forget it, eh?"

"I'd forgotten."

"Good; well, let me show you around a little. It's not such a big place, but built like a gem. Everything a man could need. A paradise, Earl. A literal paradise."

One with a serpent. As they neared the end of the corridor a tall, metallic shape stepped towards them, halting to block their path.

"Man Arbush, you left your work without permission."

"I wanted to meet a friend."

"It is noted."

"A special occasion. I didn't think anyone would mind."

"You have also failed to cleanse yourself. That too was noted."

"I was in a hurry." Arbush glanced at the yellow flecks on his arms. "Anyway I moved my quota."

The Monitor turned a little. "Man Dumarest, you will report for duty at sector 92 at the third bell. Appropriate clothing will be supplied. You will establish your residence in room 731. During your period of work, you will not carry the symbol of your rank."

The knife about which Arbush had obviously lied, a pretence which he must have thought important.

Dumarest said, "That is not possible. Never is a person of my station devoid of the insignia of his rank."

"You will not carry it to your place of work." The flat drone precluded all possibility of argument, of appeal.

Arbush grunted as the Monitor moved away.

"The fly in the ointment, Earl. Those damn things act as police. You do as they say—or else."

"Or else, what?"

"They make you. They can do it, too. I had a little trouble on my third day—some character in the gymnasium said something I didn't like. I was about to flatten him when a Monitor grabbed me. I was like a child."

"The knife," said Dumarest. "Why—"

"But you can get along," said Arbush quickly, a little too loud. "All you have to do is cooperate. I'm slow in learning, but I'm catching on. Just do your work, obey the rules and then sit back and enjoy yourself. And you keep fit, too. Look at me." He patted his waist. "In a few days, Earl, you'll be as good as new."

Perhaps, with training, exercise and a high protein diet it could be done. Would be done, no matter how long it took. As questions would be answered, mysteries explained.

Dumarest looked at the ceiling, the edges of the walls. Bright sparkles could have been inset decoration, or the glitter of minute lenses. Electronic eyes and ears, gathering and relaying information. But could an entire city be constantly monitored? And, if it was, who collected and collated the information?

Who, or what, and, above all, why?

The room was as Arbush had said, a nest of luxury by any standard; the carpets soft, the draperies rich, the furnishings of the highest quality. Alone Dumarest moved from one chamber to the other; the well-equipped bathroom, the bedroom with its wide couch, the coverings of fine material, light as gossamer, bright with abstract designs. Back in the living room, he opened the curtains and stared thoughtfully outside. The room was high, the view superb, the air clear and giving perfect vision.

He looked at the distant wall of ice, the level ground at its foot, the precise arrangement of the buildings. A city built like a gem. A complete, self-contained unit set in the wilderness.

Why?

And why had Arbush thought it necessary that he retain the knife?

An instinctive caution on first wakening, perhaps? The minstrel was shrewd, experienced in the devious ways of divergent cultures; it would have been natural for him to seek an advantage. To retain access to a weapon. Had softness later changed him?

Dumarest remembered the conversation over the wine, the enthusiasm which had accompanied every step of the tour which Arbush had conducted. To him, the city had fulfilled an ancient yearning.

"Instone," he murmured. "Instone."

"The name of the city," said a voice behind him. "Do you find it such a wonderful sound?"

She had entered silently and stood, tall and splendid in a gown of gold-laced crimson; golden sparkles on the veil of gossamer which wreathed her hair.

"Your door was open," she said. "I took it as an invitation."

A lie, the door had not been open: but it could not be locked. Custom made that unnecessary; a room was a private place not to be entered without invitation. A custom she had broken and, in so doing, had revealed herself.

"You're Eloise," he said.

"And you are Earl Dumarest." She came towards him hands extended, palms outward, fingers upright. As he placed the flat of his own palms against hers she said, "Welcome to Instone. Did Arbush tell you about me?"

"Your name, nothing else."

"I'm glad of that. It gives us something to talk about, a chance to get to know each other. Are you going to offer me something to drink?"

"I have nothing to offer."

"A deficit quickly remedied." She crossed the room to where a ledge protruded from the wall, a hatch above it. "This isn't a terminal, you'll find those in the corridors and assembly rooms; but this is how you get food and drink if you want to remain alone." Placing the flat of her palm on the ledge she said, "Eloise. Room 731. Red wine and two glasses."

She drank quickly as he sipped his own, and he guessed that she had already had enough. There was a sparkle to her eyes, a flush to her cheeks, a restless impatience which consumed her.

"Do you always identify yourself when ordering?"

"Always."

He remembered Dras; the same placing of the palm, the announcing of a name. A check on palm print and identity. A means to tally what was asked for, and the information demanded.

"Earl, we have a lot in common. Like you, I'm a stranger here. I wasn't born in the city. Tell me, what did it feel like to be falling?"

"You saw?"

"I was on the upper platform. I had a feeling, an instinct, call it what you like. I was searching the barrier and saw you. There are instruments," she said, anticipating his doubt, "Telescopes. Luck guided me to look at that spot, where you were. I watched as you were rescued. Tell me, what did it feel like when you fell?"

A rush of air, the numbing certainty of imminent death and then the shock, as something impacted his chest, the instant oblivion.

He said, "How did you get here?"

"An accident." She poured herself more wine, frowned at his barely touched glass. "I'm a dancer. On Lamack, I joined up with an entrepreneur who formed a small troupe and brought us here to Camollard. There's a city, Breen, and we made out for a while. Then he had a bright idea. There were rumours of a city far to the north and he guessed that, in such a place, we would be popular. He bought a flyer and we started toward it. A storm rose and we got lost. Finally, we crashed."

"Here?"

"A mile away, on the ice. I was lucky. Adara, a friend, you'll meet him later, saw what had happened. He persuaded Camolsaer to send out Monitors and he went with them. It took half a day to find me. The others were all dead." Pausing she added, "That was five years ago."

"Camollard," he said thoughtfully. "The name of this world. Do you have the coordinates?"

An unexpected question which caused her to frown. Then, face clearing, she smiled. "Of course, the warp; you don't know where you are. I haven't the coodinates, but Camollard is close to the Elmirha Dust. You can see it from the southern hemisphere."

A half million light years from Tynar—the warp had thrown them far.

"Are there ships?"

"Not many, and those that call land at Breen. It's a small place on the equator. There's a mine working a seam of thorenite, but mostly they hunt. Furs and the fruit of doltchel. A small plant growing in sheltered nooks. It's a narcotic."

A bleak world with but a single town, a single space field. Such worlds were common.

She said, "You aren't drinking, Earl. Have I offended you?"

Caution she decided, as he shook his head. Such a man would always be cautious. Careful of each step he took until he was sure of where he was going, and then nothing would stop him. A man who had come in answer to her prayer. A strong man, hard, ruthless; she could tell it by the set of his mouth, the line of his jaw. Her eyes dropped to the knife in his boot. A knife was nothing, a strip of edged and pointed steel; substitutes could be made from a broken bottle, a host of items—by itself a blade was harmless, certainly against the Monitors which was possibly why Camolsaer had allowed it. Allowed it—unaware that it wasn't the knife which was dangerous, but the man.

Her man, she had known it from the first. One way or another, he would be hers.

He said, "How do you get from here to Breen?"

"You don't."

"Can't?"

"Both. There is no contact with any other city. No ships, no flyers, nothing. Instone is isolated; a vague rumour which no one will ever take the trouble to investigate. Even if you could climb the wall, there would still be the Krim to contend with. Savage animals who roam the ice."

"We saw them—they were men."

"Or things which looked like men," she corrected. "When they get too close, Camolsaer sends the Monitors out against them. If you tried to escape it would send them against you."

"Escape?"

"Escape, Earl. Haven't you grasped it yet? This isn't just a city, it's a jail. A prison in which we're all under sentence of death. And you, Earl; you'll be one of the first to go!"

Chapter Ten

~~~~~~~~~~~~~~~~~~~~~~~~~~~~~~~~~~~~

The work was a mindless routine, taking packets from a machine to where others would feed them into different machines. Made work, unessential, something to occupy the time of humans while machines ran the city. Machines and Camolsaer, who controlled them.

At the bell Dumarest returned to his room, changed, and continued his inspection of the city. It had lasted more than a week; a close scrutiny of every available chamber and compartment, each corridor and passage on the entire complex.

If Instone was a prison, he was determined to find a way out. And it was a prison; in that the woman, though hysterical, had been right. Without roads, contact with other places, a means to cross the ice, it could be nothing else.

"Earl!" A man called to him as he entered the gymnasium. "Care to wrestle?"

"Later perhaps."

"I was telling Sagen about that throw you showed me." The man was insistent. "He's willing to bet a turn of duty that you couldn't best him within five minutes."

A bet he would surely lose. The men were soft, untoughened by hard labor, afraid to hurt or to receive pain. Dumarest stripped off his tunic and moved to the center of the area. Sagen, grimly determined, took up his stance.

A bad position, the hands too widely separated, the feet too close. A feint and he would be off-balance, an easy prey, the bout over within seconds. But Dumarest had no intention of winning. It was time he made a friend, and this was a good opportunity.

He moved in, carelessly, open to be seized. Sagen took the proffered opportunity, hands gripping, closing; body

99

turning as he attempted the throw. Dumarest resisted, converted the direction of applied force to his own advantage, attacked in turn. Sagen staggered, barely recovered and moved cautiously, eyes reflecting the knowledge of his near-defeat. He came in again, and this time Dumarest did not resist.

The man who had called to him grunted his annoyance as Dumarest's shoulders hit the floor.

"You win, Sagen. Earl wasn't as good as I thought."

A conviction the instructor didn't share. Later, over a cup of tisane, he said, "You let me win, Earl. Why?"

"You're the instructor. You have to be the best."

"I'm not and you know it." Sagen frowned into his cup. "You could take my place at any time. Camolsaer would approve it."

"Perhaps." Dumarest wasn't so sure. "You're doing a good job, Sagen. I wouldn't have the patience. There's something you can tell me, though. I've been taking a look around the city. What lies below the lower region?"

"The power plant, waste converters and artesian wells." Sagen didn't hesitate over the answer. "There are shafts delving into the crust to heat and thaw the permafrost."

"Anyone working down there?"

"Only machines. Machines and the Monitors, of course."

"And Camolsaer?"

"Yes, I guess so."

"Guess?"

"I'm not certain. No one ever goes into the lower regions. I suppose, after conversion, you'd get a chance; but not before."

Conversion, the word used instead of death, but conversion into what? Eloise would tell him, but Dumarest knew better than to take what she said at face value.

He said, "Tell me about Camolsaer."

"Camolsaer?" Sagen seemed baffled. "It—well—it runs the city."

"I know that; but the name, where did that come from?"

"A contraction. Computer Analogue Maintenance Of Life Support And Environmental Resources." Something Eloise hadn't known; Arbush too indifferent to discover. "It controls things. It feeds us, clothes us, keeps us warm. It—it's Camolsaer."

God spelled with a different name, at least as far as the inhabitants of Instone were concerned. A mysterious, invisible, unknown entity which had governed their lives from the moment of birth. And before. Only with the permission of Camolsaer could children be bred—the special diet devoid of sterility drugs obtained.

A lifetime of conditioning, in which absolute reliance was placed on the voice coming from the terminals. Absolute dependency achieved by fact and custom.

Finishing his tisane Sagen said, "You're new here, Earl, and I guess it's natural for you to be curious; but anything you want to know can be learned from Camolsaer. Just ask at one of the terminals. There's plenty of them around."

"Thank you," said Dumarest. "I will."

"I'll be getting back to the gymnasium." Sagen rose to his feet. "It's always pretty busy at a time like this. Young bucks wanting to learn tricks and build up some muscle. Whenever a Knelling's due it's the same. Don't forget, now; just ask what you want to know. You can even get a prediction on—" He broke off, looking at Dumarest's expression. "Something wrong?"

"No. Did you say you can get a prediction?"

"That's right." The instructor lifted a careless hand. "See you around."

Alone, Dumarest sat and sipped slowly at his tisane. Any man or machine in possession of all the facts could make a simple prediction; but the word had unpleasant associations. Predictions were the area in which cybers excelled. Was Instone an extension of the Cyclan? An experiment started and later abandoned?

A girl, young, laughing, walked past him on her way to a terminal, there to ask a question about the whereabouts of her lover. Dumarest ignored her as he ignored the others in the chamber, the brightly dressed men and women, some of whom looked at him with interest. To them he was a novelty, something strange, intriguing.

Arbush came towards him, his gilyre strung over his shoulders, two girls hanging on his arms.

"Earl, a message. Eloise expects you at her room tonight." He moved on, a contented man; accepting the surface of things and not bothering about their cause. Indifferent to the clues at hand.

The name, the city, the thing which ran it.

Instone—Installation One.

A scientific project built as a complete unit and set in the midst of a hostile waste, to ensure isolation. And, if it was the first, there could be others placed on remote worlds circling lonely suns.

Perhaps the Cyclan had built it, perhaps not; many worlds bore the traces of early settlers eager to construct civilizations to their own pattern, to create Utopias which would solve all the ills which plagued Mankind. And, on the face of it, Instone was a Utopia; classless, with an even distribution of available goods, no law but the ubiquitous Monitors, no rule but the dictates of Camolsaer. But to exist for any length of time a Utopia had to be static, and the Cyclan would know that. A thing which went against their creed of progressive domination. A testing ground then, for some long-range purpose? A breeding chamber. A culture which could be directed and controlled by the remorseless pressures of necessity and logic.

A mystery, and one he couldn't answer; but if the Cyclan had built it he had fallen right into their hands.

Eloise had never seemed more beautiful. Watching her from where he sat beneath the window, Adara felt again the jealous hurt which had now become all too familiar. She no longer needed him. Now she had found another on whom to lean.

He looked on as she handed Dumarest a goblet of wine. Tonight she wore diaphanous veils, her feet bare, ankles adorned with bands holding tiny bells. More bands graced her wrists, small sounds tinkling as she moved. Her hair was loose, a rippling waterfall which caught the light and reflected it as if it had been oil. Her breasts, half-bared, were dusted with motes of gold.

Dumarest noticed his attention.

He said, quietly, "Your friend is jealous. You should not ignore him."

"Adara?" She smiled, white teeth flashing between scarlet lips. "He's a friend."

A friend and more, a lover certainly; and such a man could be dangerous. Dumarest examined him from behind the cover of his wine. A body which was too soft, a face too worn. A man old before his time, lines creasing his cheeks; his eyes shadowed by sleepless rest, haunted. He

drank too deep and too often, like a man seeking an anodyne for an inner pain.

Drink enough and heated emotions would suggest an
answer to his problem.

"Forget him, Earl. Drink your wine. Arbush, give us a
tune."

The minstrel grinned and slapped the rump of one of
his attendant girls.

"My instrument, girl. Hurry!"

The air throbbed as he touched the strings, musing with
the skill of long practice, building anticipation as he
strummed a succession of chords.

"What shall it be? A love song? No, we have too much
love. A wistful air of a young girl betrayed by her lover?
No, here that particular type of hell does not exist. One of
unrequited passion, perhaps? Of adventure? Of bold men
venturing into the spaces between the stars?" The strumming grew deep, strong; the pulse of an engine, the empty
gulfs, a beat like that of a pounding heart.

"No." Eloise stood in the center of the room; the others
pressed back against the wall, some sitting, others squatted
on the carpet. Ten of them; those whom Dumarest had
met, friends of Adara and the woman, Arbush's girls.

"Follow me, minstrel." Lifting her arms her fingers began to touch; thin, high ringings coming from the tiny
cymbals she had slipped on her fingers and thumbs. "We
are in a tavern," she whispered. "A hot and smoky place,
heavy with the scent of wine. You know such places and
know what is played there. Play, minstrel. Play as I
dance."

The thrumming of the strings settled, became a repeti-
tious background against which the tap of whispering
drums echoed; chords rising to match the swaying undula-
tions of the woman, accompanying the thin ringings of the
cymbals, the bells at wrists and ankles.

It was a dance as old as time, performed with consum-
mate skill; flesh and bone moving in suggestive abandon,
naked feet with crimson nails caressing the carpet, the
waterfall of hair a shimmering cloud of erotic beauty.

The lights seemed to fade, the walls to fall away, the
watchers to turn into a circle of watching eyes, hands
moving, fingers tapping as they followed the rhythm;
bodies responding to the invitation explicit in every gesture, the thrust and sway of hips, waist, breasts, thighs. So

women had danced in primordial times, offering themselves to a surrogate of the Earth God; a ritual designed to make the ground fertile, the harvest good.

Now aimed at one man alone.

Adara sensed it and gulped down his wine. Arbush knew it and smiled as his spatulate fingers danced over the strings; the tips hitting the sounding board, returning to alter the note, moving with a fluid grace. Dumarest felt it and wondered what lay behind the bribe, the offer of her flesh.

She wanted something—that had been obvious from the beginning. She had met him too often by apparent chance for it to have been an accident. And there had been hints, barely concealed; suggestions half made, as if she were waiting for him to discover something.

The dance ended and she came to sit on the floor at his feet. Arbush began to play again, this time accompanying himself with a song; a ballad more fitted to a spaceman's dive than to any decent company, but no one seemed to find it offensive. The girls who had accompanied him danced in turn; neat, precise little movements, smooth enough but awkward when compared to the previous display.

"We need more wine," Eloise decided. "Adara, order more wine."

He rose to his feet and came towards her and Dumarest saw that, despite what he had drunk, he was coldly sober.

"Eloise, is that wise? Already you have had more than enough."

"Are you telling me what to do?"

He winced at the coldness of her voice. "No, but—"

"Then order it! Damn you, order it or do I have to do it myself?"

"Eloise, you're mad. Ever since Earl came, you've been acting strange. Don't you realize what you're doing?"

"I'm living!" she flared. "Don't you understand? Living! For the first time in years I've met a real man, and to hell with you and everything else. Get me some more wine!"

A man rose and quietly left the room. Another followed, one of Arbush's girls. Rats, she thought bleakly, getting out while the going was good; not wanting to be contaminated with Eloise's presence, associated with her disregard.

Two women remained. One of them said, "Earl, I can be found in room 532."

"Get out!" snapped Eloise. "Do your hunting somewhere else."

"If you've any sense, Earl, you'll join me." Without further comment she left, her companion close behind.

Arbush plucked at a string. "The end of the party," he said regretfully. "And I was just beginning to enjoy it. That dance took me back. There was a girl who danced as you did. A vision of delight, who took all I had and left me for another with more. Well, such is life. A man can only be thankful for such pleasures, transient though they may be."

"A harlot," she sneered. "Is that what you think I am?"

Again he plucked the string and, as the singing note died, said quietly, "I did not say that you were—but if you are not, then you are unique among all the dancers I have ever known."

"You fat bastard!" She rose, fingers like claws. "I'll have your eyes for that! Earl, do you believe what he says?"

"Does it matter?"

"It matters! Dear God, it matters! I love you! Can't you understand? I love you!"

It had come, as he had known it would. Adara looked at his hands and found, to his surprise, that they did not tremble. The inner hurt was gone also, as if emotion had been raised to too high a pitch, to burn itself out and leave only ashes. Would the Knelling be like this? Would he, once his number had been tolled, feel the same cold, detached resignation?

He stared in surprise at the glass of wine thrust into his hand, the man who had placed it there.

"Sit down," said Dumarest. "Sit and drink your wine."

A kindness, the consideration of the victor for the vanquished; would he have been capable of such a gesture? Adara sat and drank and said, "Earl, I think there is something you should know."

"Adara! You—"

"Be quiet!" snapped Dumarest, not looking at the woman. To Adara he said, "Why were you so insistent that Eloise should not order more wine?"

"It is noted. Everything you order is noted. If anyone is

considered to be guilty of too great an excess, it tells
against them."

"And?"

"I can answer that." Eloise stepped forward with a delicate chiming of bells. "Drink too much, use too many
drugs, eat like a pig, have too much sex, pick a fight or
fail to cooperate—it all tells against you. Do it too often
and you'll draw a low number at the Knelling. You know
what the Knelling is? Hasn't anyone told you yet? It's
when the unfit are culled. The unfit according to Camolsaer, of course; that damned god in a box who rules this
jail. And it is a jail, Earl; surely you have discovered that
for yourself by now. A prison from which there is only one
way out." Her lifted hand made a cutting gesture at her
throat. "Curtains. Finish. Food for the worms."

Arbush said, dryly, "A pleasant prospect. Is there anything else?"

"When you get too old. When you fall too sick. When
you become too anti-social, whatever that means in this
godforsaken place. When you don't fit the nice, neat, tidy
pattern laid down by God knows who." She glared at him.
"You won't last long. You like wine too much, have too
many girls. You dodge work and go your own way. And
you're too fat."

"I like my comforts."

"Sure, and you'll pay for them. With your life."

As she would also, of that she was certain. Again, she
had allowed emotion to ruin the carefully maintained appearance of calm. But now, at least, there was a hope.

"Earl, please, you've got to get me away from here."

"Got to? Why?"

"Because I love you." It wasn't reason enough; she had
given him words, nothing else, and how many other
women had told him the same? Too many others. Enough
for him to have learned that what is said and what is
meant are not the same thing. She added, "And, because
in a way, I saved your life. If I hadn't been watching and
spotted you against the barrier, the Monitors could never
have reached you in time."

"Is that true, Adara?"

"Yes, Earl. I was with her at the time. I—she reported
it to Camolsaer and insisted that aid be sent."

"Insisted?" If Dumarest had noticed the slip, he gave no
indication of it. "Can anyone insist?"

"No, but you can make a point on the basis of logic. Camolsaer stated that, as you had come from the ice, you had to be Krim and therefore destroyed. I pointed out that the Krim are animals and animals do not use ropes to descend a cliff. Therefore, you had to be men and should be rescued."

Rescued and healed; but where was the logic in that if he was fated to be selected for death?

"We've got to escape, Earl." Eloise was insistent. "You've got to find a way." And then, as he remained silent, she added, "Are you wondering why Camolsaer saved you? I'll tell you—for raw materials. The fabric of your brain can be used to build more Monitors. That's what conversion means. Your body reduced to basic elements to be used as fertilizer; your brain trimmed and fitted into a machine. The fools here think they move on up to a higher level of existence, but they're wrong. The ego doesn't remain, it can't. Would you ever take a Monitor for a man?"

"Eloise!"

"Shut up, Adara! I've told you this before and I thought you believed me. But you're weak. You know what must happen and yet do nothing about it. Remember the last Knelling? I saw your face and knew what you felt, but afterwards? You did nothing. You just slipped back into the routine. Acting a part, pretending to be a good little boy so as not to be punished. And yet you have the gall to call yourself a man."

"That's enough!" Dumarest stepped between them as Adara rose, his face flushed at the insult. "Eloise, Adara is your friend. You should remember that."

"Earl!"

"A friend," he repeated coldly. "Not a toy to be thrown aside at a whim."

A rebuke which she deserved and, looking at him, she guessed why Dumarest had made it. Adara was a resident of the city, a source of information and a potential enemy. A rejected lover who could ruin any plan they chose to make. Elementary caution dictated that he be treated with consideration. Why hadn't she thought of that?

Brooding over his gilyre Arbush said, "I think we are becoming excited without need. Eloise has drunk too much wine. You have done nothing to offend Camolsaer, Earl. You are not old or fat or greedy. You are not, as I am, tempted by the lures of the flesh. There is no reason why you should be chosen." He plucked a string. "I think that the woman is more concerned for herself than for you."

"Yes," she admitted. "I am concerned for myself. And so would you be, in my place. But you're wrong about Earl not being in danger. Among these people he is a wolf among sheep. A source of contamination. How long will it be before he gains a following? A man who could survive as he has done will never willingly submit to the Knell. He will fight and, if nothing else, set an example of resistance. If I can see it, then so must Camolsaer."

"True." Arbush thoughtfully plucked another string. "Earl is a most unusual man."

"And because of that most likely to be chosen," said Adara. "Eloise is right in what she says. There is every—" He broke off, turning, his face suddenly haggard as a Monitor strode into the room. "What do you want?"

The thing ignored him, coming to a halt before the little group; the head moving from side to side, a ruby glow behind the elongated planes of crystal which were its eyes. The paint on its metal mask was a parody of a human visage.

"Man Dumarest, you will take this."

It extended an arm, a slip of card held in the hand; an appendage larger than normal, made of overlapping plates, the ends of the fingers tipped with a grey plastic.

"Man Adara. Man Arbush."

Two other slips.

"Woman Eloise."

The fourth and last. As the Monitor left the room she looked at it; her laughter hard, brittle, taut with incipient hysteria.

"Number nine. The last time it was number twenty-two. Adara?"

"Thirteen."

"I'm number seven," said Arbush. "How about you, Earl?"

Dumarest looked at the slip. It held an abstract design over which was printed a bold figure one.

"The prime!" Eloise sucked in her breath. "I told you, Earl. You'll be the first to go!"

Chapter Eleven

For a long moment there was silence and then Arbush rose, crossed to the serving hatch and, placing his hand flat on the plate said, loudly, "Arbush. Wine to room 638. Four decanters."

He carried them, two in each hand, back to where they sat; Dumarest thoughtful, the woman excited, Adara slumped in resigned despair.

"Drink," he said. "It is an unusual occasion. Not every day does a man receive official notification of his impending demise." The wine made liquid gurglings as he poured. Handing each a glass, he raised his own. "A toast. To optimism!"

Dumarest sipped at his wine, knowing that the toast was badly chosen. They needed more than optimism. He said, "How long?"

"Until the Knelling?" Eloise bit at her lower lip, the bruised flesh a vivid scarlet against the pallor of her cheeks. "Three days. The first is a period of calm, the last a time of waiting. In between, those with high numbers do their best to remain safe; those with low try to alter the odds."

She saw his frown and hastened to explain.

"Everyone gets a number, but no one knows for sure how many are to be Knelled. It could be a couple of dozen, in which case those with numbers above, say, twenty stand a chance. If five are culled before the critical period, the bell will only toll nineteen times." She added, bleakly, "But no one knows for certain how many Camolsaer will take. And you, the prime, will have no chance at all."

Not unless the full number should be killed before the last day. And even then, there was no assurance of safety.

Dumarest leaned back, eyes shadowed with thought, assessing the problem, its cause.

The city was a closed unit; each birth meant that there had to be a matching death. The time in which aggression was allowed a crude device, to ensure the survival of the fittest. Crude because it would never be allowed to work to its logical end. He could kill a hundred men and still be taken; a man too dangerous to be allowed to survive. Only the pretence was provided, the illusion which gave birth to a modicum of strength. He remembered the gymnasium, Sagen's comment. Young men training in order to defend themselves. Older men stiffening muscles, ready for the anticipated encounters.

"Do the Monitors interfere?"

"Not during the actual time of combat," said Adara quickly. "But you must realize that many people form protective groupings. Most stay in their rooms."

"The doors?"

"Blocked." Adara glanced towards the couch in the bedroom, the furnishings. "On the final day there is, of course, no combat. Then people get together to wait or to enjoy themselves in various ways. To drink, take drugs, make love." He glanced at the woman. "Other things."

"A pity." Absently, Arbush picked up his gilyre and ran the tips of his fingers over the strings. "A life so pleasant, so full of ease, to be so quickly ended. If I were allowed to die a natural death, I would stay here to the end of my days. Even as it is, there is a chance. A score of men to die. More if necessary, and once again to relax and take what is offered." He lifted one broad hand and clenched the spatulate fingers. "Earl, shall we show Camolsaer how it should be done?"

"You're a fool!" snapped Eloise. "Do you think they will wait to be butchered? And after, even if you did survive, what of the next time?"

Dumarest said, ignoring the interjection, "Adara, are weapons provided?"

"No."

"Are they allowed?"

"Only if self-provided." He glanced at the knife showing above Dumarest's boot. "You will have an advantage. None could stand against you—if they allowed you to get within reach."

Had he been allowed to retain the weapon as an example? Or had it been a test, to see what the introduction of a new element would do to the carefully nurtured residents of the city? Something in the nature of a virus to test the resistance of the culture it contained.

A question which now could be safely ignored. He watched as the minstrel gave Adara more wine. The man seemed numbed, drinking like an automaton, unnerved by the shocks he had received. A fatal attitude which would make him willingly accept what was to come, welcoming it, perhaps, as an anodyne to his loss.

"Earl." Eloise moved, crouching at his feet, her arms wrapped around his legs. "We haven't much time, darling. What are you going to do?"

"What can he do?" Adara blinked, the wine he had taken finally having its effect. "What can anyone do? We are here and that's all there is to it. When the Knell sounds and the Monitors come, all we can do is to submit gracefully."

"You—not I!"

"Eloise! Please, I need you."

A cry from the heart, a man faced with the sure knowledge of oblivion and not knowing which way to turn. A child reaching out for a familiar comfort.

Dumarest said, "Go with him, Eloise. Take him to his room. Put him to bed."

"Earl! You ask me to do that!"

"That and more if necessary," he said harshly. "He saved your life, remember? You owe it to him to provide what comfort you can."

"But, Earl, I love you."

"And what does that mean?" He met her eyes, saw the bruised hurt they contained, the bafflement. "Does it mean that, because you say it, I must love you in return? That I have to make an enemy of a man who has done me no harm? Damn it, woman, grow up!"

She stiffened, face reflecting her anger, her hurt pride; and then, glancing at Adara where he sat, she softened and rose.

"You're right, Earl. Adara has been good to me. But I meant what I said. I love you. I shall always love you. I don't want you ever to forget that."

The room was a clot of shadows; pale starlight, coming from the window in the other chamber, doing little more than haze the darkness; making the bed a darker mound among others, the door itself a pale oblong in which something stood.

Dumarest rolled, one hand slipping the knife from his boot; rising poised to strike.

"Please!" The voice was a high, breathless whisper. "Earl, is that you? Please say something if you're awake."

It was the woman from the party, the one who had invited him to her room. She stepped back as he drew near, her eyes wide, terrified as they looked at the knife. She gulped as he slid it back into his boot.

"You—I thought you were going to kill me!"

"Is it allowed?"

"Not yet. Not until dawn. But you wouldn't kill me, Earl, would you. Not when there are other things to do. So much more pleasant things."

She had retreated at his advance to stand before the window, pale starlight on her hair, the blonde tresses shimmering as if dusted with silver. A tall, proud, sensuous animal; he remembered how her eyes had clung to him, the naked invitation she had offered.

"What do you want?"

"You, Earl. You can stay with me in my room until the Knelling. You are the prime and deserve the best. I shall give it to you. Anything you want will be yours. All I can offer will ease those last hours until the bell."

Her face held an expression he had seen before. The feral anticipation of sensuous delight; the titivation of yielding to the demands of a man who would no longer have cause to restrain his appetite. Such creatures were to be found at every arena, harpies feeding on overstimulated emotion; willing to be degraded, humiliated, eager to pander to every bestial desire.

"Earl?"

He said, coldly, "I'll take you to your room. If I see you again I'll kill you. You had better believe that."

"You filth!" Anger thinned her lips, tightened the skin of her face so that it looked like scraped bone in the cold light of the stars. "You—"

"Get out! Now!"

A woman scorned, the second in a few hours; but where she could be ignored, Eloise could not. Outside in the corridor Dumarest tensed, listening. He heard the soft pad of running feet, a cry, the sound of a scuffle. Turning a corner he caught a glimpse of a running shape; another lying on the floor, groaning, blood making a pool beneath the shoulders.

The woman had lied. The first day had passed, already the violence had begun.

As he stepped towards the groaning man, a Monitor stepped before him.

"Man Dumarest, this is not your concern."

"The man is hurt."

"The man is dying. He will be attended to."

Other Monitors joined the first, stooping to pick up the injured man. Dumarest followed them to where a passage slanted towards the lower levels. It opened on a chamber containing a closed door. As he watched it swung wide, to reveal a corridor bright with a pale blue luminescence. Before he could enter, the door slammed in his face.

One of the ubiquitous Monitors appeared at its side.

"Man Dumarest, this area is forbidden. Return to the level above."

Up past the assembly rooms now deserted, the pool filled with idle water, the gymnasium empty of exercising men.

Dumarest reached a door, knocked, waited, knocked again.

"Who is it?"

"Arbush, open up!"

The minstrel was cautious. From behind the closed panel came the sound of scraping, then the door cracked open to reveal an eye.

"Earl!" He swung open the door. "Eloise lied to us," he complained. "She said there would be a day of calm. Calm, hell! A bunch of young thugs tried to jump me. I got one and the others ran. What happened to you?"

"I've been resting. Asleep."

"Thinking?" Arbush was shrewd. "Earl, did you—"

"Bring your gilyre," interrupted Dumarest. "I think Eloise would like to hear you play."

Like the minstrel she had blocked her door, opening it only when she was certain of who stood outside. Adara was with her, his face pale, his eyes haunted with inner trepidation. A decanter of wine, untouched, stood on a small table at his side.

"Earl!" He rose, hands extended, the palms outward to

be touched. "It's good of you to call. This is a bad time to be alone."

"I thought you'd like some music," said Dumarest. "Arbush, play something loud and cheerful. Very loud and very cheerful."

"Something like this, Earl?" The minstrel's fingers danced on the strings, notes rising, high, shrill, seeming to hang and quiver in the air; resonance building so that the glasses on the tray rang in sympathy.

"A neat tune, is it not?" Arbush winked as he played. "I composed it during a time on Helada, when I was invited to stay as a guest at the court of King Swendle. There was a girl, a veritable flower, but the old man was jealous and had set electronic guards. Even so, we managed to talk and arrange an assignation. I learned later that his electrician had been whipped for his failure to maintain his equipment." His voice lowered, became urgent. "Talk, Earl. While I play, nothing can overhear us."

Dumarest wasted no time.

"Adara. When you went out to rescue Eloise, how did you travel? Did you walk or fly?"

"Fly, but why do you ask? What—"

"Never mind the questions. You flew. With the same attachments as the Monitors use?"

"Yes."

"Where did you get them?"

"The Monitors provided the unit. They got it from a store close to the northern exit."

"And the weapons they use against the Krim? The missile launchers. The same place?"

"I'm not sure. I—," Adara frowned, then his face cleared. "Yes. I remember now. The Monitors armed themselves before we set out. They took the weapons from the same store."

Eloise whispered, her breath warm against his cheek, "Earl! Do you have a plan?"

A bare idea formed while he had lain resting, thinking; correlating every scrap of information he had gained about the city and its occupants.

"A chance," he admitted, "but the only one we've got. We can't cross the ice on foot. Even if we could cross the ground beyond the city, we could never scale the barrier. And if we could do that we'd never make it to Breen. There could be tunnels running from the lower levels, in fact there have to be; but we'd still have to dig our way to the surface. Flying is the only way out."

"Simple," she said, disappointed. "All we have to do is to get the units and go. But what about the Monitors? Camolsaer? As soon as we touch the store, it would know about it."

"Perhaps."

"It can't be done, Earl." Adara shook his head. "The Monitors would order us away."

"What if they do? Do you have to obey?" Dumarest saw the man blink, as if at an unheard of concept. "Listen, Adara, unquestioning obedience is the badge of slavery. If ever you get away from here, you'll have to learn how to be free. You may as well start now. I suppose you do want to get away?"

Adara hesitated, looking at Eloise.

"I'm going," she said firmly. "I don't care what you do, Adara, but I'm going. If you want to stay here and listen to that damned bell knell away your life, you're welcome."

"It isn't death," he said weakly. "It's—"

"Conversion. I know. If you want it you can have it. Me, I'd rather take my chances on a different kind of hell. What do you want us to do, Earl?"

"Get tools from the workshops. Levers, hammers, wedges; anything to force open that store. Can you do it?"

"No." Adara was positive. "The Monitors would stop us."

"Normally, yes," agreed Dumarest. "But times aren't normal. Men are out in the corridors hunting each other down. At any other time the Monitors would stop it, but not now. This is the one chance we have of breaking free. If you take the tools and anything tries to stop you—well, don't be stopped. It's your life, remember. Eloise, you've worked in the gardens, can you get chemicals?"

"Such as?"

"Artificial fertilizers."

"No. The stuff comes through pipes in monitored amounts."

A pity; with fertilizer and sugar he could have made a crude but powerful bomb. But there were other ways. Keeping his voice below the singing thrum of the strings he said, "This is what you must do. Get tools and take them to the store. When the moment comes, wrench it open and take out flying units and weapons."

"And?" Eloise met his eyes. "Don't try to con me, Earl," she said. "It isn't as simple as that. If it was, you wouldn't need help. What else must we do?"

"Create a diversion. More than one if possible. Start some fires, well away from the store."

"Fires?" Adara looked blank. "How? What with?"

"I know how," said Eloise. "I was in a house once—well, never mind. But I can start a fire. How about him?" She jerked her head at the minstrel. "What will he be doing?"

"Helping me."

"And you?"

"Me?" Dumarest shrugged. "I'm going to stop the bell."

Corridor 137 was deserted, the door to the room in which Dumarest had woken locked. He knocked, waited, knocked again; then slipped the knife from his boot and thrust it into the crack. A heave and the door opened with a brittle snap of metal. Dras was nowhere to be seen. He appeared from an inner compartment as Dumarest tore at the casing of the diagnostic machine.

"What are you doing?" He stared, voice rising into a scream. "How dare you touch that machine. Help! Monitors! To—"

He sagged as Arbush slammed a fist against his jaw, the minstrel catching him as he fell. Without a word, he heaved the body back into the inner room and rested the unconscious man on a couch.

"I was sorry to do that," he murmured as he returned to where Dumarest was working. "In a way he saved our lives. Well, it can't be helped." He sucked at a split knuckle. "Need any help, Earl?"

Dumarest shook his head. The inside of the machine lay bare; a mass of electronic wizardry into which he probed with questing fingers. As he'd guessed there was a communication unit installed into the machine, a radio-link with Camolsaer. He adjusted it, altering the circuits, seeing tiny sparks flare between poorly made connections. Satisfied, he stepped back into the corridor.

"Get back to the others," he told Arbush. "Help them. But not yet. First, we have work to do."

Part of it was done; the readjusted machine was now broadcasting a band of white noise, a stream of static which, he hoped, would disturb the close contact each

Monitor had with the others and Camolsaer. A distraction to add to the others, but this one with a more definite purpose.

"Now!"

Dumarest ran down the corridor, Arbush close behind him, a glinting instrument in his hand. A heavy testing device he had taken from the instrument table in the ward. As a Monitor came into sight Dumarest slowed, half-turned, went down as Arbush viciously smashed the tool against his head. It was skillfully done. The blow was struck at the last moment, tearing the flesh at the side of the neck, the lobe of the ear. A minor wound which provided plenty of blood.

As the Monitor advanced with two others, the minstrel turned and ran back the way he had come.

Dumarest didn't move.

He lay, eyes closed, breathing shallowly; a man unconscious from a blow which had apparently crushed the back of his skull. He felt hands grip him, lift him; a soft humming as the Monitors carried him away from where he had fallen. Through slitted eyes he saw the overhead lights pass, the corridor narrow, the roof descend as his bearers moved to a lower level. Camolsaer would have known of what had happened in the ward; but the radio disturbance would prevent communication with the Monitors who carried him and they, obeying previous commands, would take him where he wanted to go.

Into the sealed, lower regions of the city.

Into the heart of Camolsaer itself.

He closed his eyes as the Monitors halted, sagging limp in their grasp; hearing the soft sigh of an opening door, feeling the touch of cold air. When next he looked he saw a pale blue luminescence which came from the walls, roof and floor; a shadowless glow he had seen before. A dozen yards and he was dropped on a bench. As he heard the pad of retreating feet, he turned his head and looked around.

He was in a small room, the sides lined with triple tiers of bunks. Two were occupied, one with a man, the other with a woman; both unconscious, neither dead. The woman stirred as he touched her, moaning, one hand lifting as if to protect herself. One side of her temple was bruised, the broken skin oozing blood. The man had been struck with something long and hard, the white of splintered bone showing at the angle of his jaw. When touched, he didn't move.

Victims of the pre-knelling, collected for later conversion as he had been himself. Dumarest tried to remember if the man was the one he had seen struck down, but couldn't be sure. There would be other rooms, or maybe the man had already been processed.

But he was not here to save the fallen.

The room had no door; only an arched opening which led to the wide passage outside. Dumarest stepped towards it, halting as he reached the opening. A Monitor stood outside.

It was very still; pale blue light bathing the metal of which it was constructed, blending with that of the wall so that the Monitor was almost invisible. Only the eyes, glowing ruby, could be clearly seen. The eyes and the paint which daubed the mask.

Red paint, yellow, fashioned to form a clown-like visage; the parody of mouth and nose. A pathetic attempt to regain lost humanity; proof positive of the residual awareness of the fragmented brain which had once known a different life.

Motionless, Dumarest studied it. The shape was obvious; trial and error over countless years had evolved the human frame into the most highly efficient general-purpose construction there was. To deviate from it would be to lose efficiency. And yet to slavishly copy it held complications.

Metal, weight for weight, was not as strong as living bone. Muscle was more compact, more versatile than any combination of wires and electro-magnets, pulleys and constructive devices. The thing was larger than a man, which meant that it had to be heavier. More weight meant less agility. Balance, once lost, would not be easily regained.

Like a fighter poised in a ring Dumarest studied his opponent, searching for points of maximum strength, places of maximum weakness.

The head, despite the paint and lensed eyes, would not hold the brain. That would be in the chest cavity, together with communication devices. The power supply would be in the stomach, lowering the center of gravity; a part of it probably in the thighs to make room for the life-support apparatus which nurtured the brain. The pads at the tips of the fingers would be sensors. The feet, also padded, would be to cushion the impact of walking, as well as to provide good traction.

The eyes then. Blinded the thing would be relatively unharmed, but sightless would be an easy victim. A mistake which Dumarest recognised, just in time. This was not a creature of flesh and blood. The eyes were crystal panes, not yielding tissue. A thrown knife might splinter one, never two; without the jarring impact of pain, the damage would be minor.

"Man Dumarest." The Monitor took one step away from the far side of the passage. "You will return to your bench and wait."

"Go to hell!"

"Your response is meaningless. Return to your bench and wait."

The flat tones had not altered, probably could not alter; but the response had carried a message all the same. Whatever humanity the thing retained was proof against insult; or perhaps it was unable to recognize or deal with flagrant disobedience.

Dumarest said, "What is your name?"

"Name?"

"What were you called when you were alive?"

"Alive?"

"When you wore flesh like mine. When you had a face instead of a metal mask. Tell me, what was your name?"

A gamble. Questions calculated to confuse and, for a moment, he thought that he had won. The Monitor swayed a little, one hand rising to touch the painted mask; then, abruptly, it seemed to stiffen.

Then, like a blur, it attacked.

Chapter Twelve

~~~~~~~~~~~~~~~~~~~~~~~~~~~~~~~~~

It was fast, too fast; mass once set into motion could not be easily controlled. Dumarest spun to one side, avoiding the reaching hand, feeling the impact numb his left shoulder. The blow threw him back against the tier of bunks, his right hand falling to touch flesh, the shape of the woman. He ducked as the Monitor turned, arms extended, hands like flails. From the grill of the mask came a flat droning.

"You will obey. You will return to your bench and wait. You will obey."

"Your name!" said Dumarest. "What is your name?"

A weakness, discovered almost by accident; a thing which seemed to disturb the Monitor. Or perhaps it was his own disobedience, something outside of the thing's experience. It would catch him, crush him perhaps; force him to the bench there to wait for others to come, to take him, to render him apart.

He stooped as the thing advanced, throwing his weight against one of the thighs, feeling the solid impact of metal against flesh and bone. A sweeping hand touched the back of his skull and filled his sight with flaring colors. Dodging behind the Monitor Dumarest raised his foot and kicked, slamming the sole of his boot into the back. A plate dented a little; otherwise he might as well have kicked a stone wall.

Heavy, too heavy to be easily thrown off-balance; and yet there had to be a way. Dodging, weaving, feeling the waft of air across his face from the flailing hands, Dumarest edged towards the opening; ducked away from it as the Monitor raced to stand guard, felt again the face of the woman beneath his hand.

She wore a loose garment, a braided jacket open at the

120

front to reveal the swell of naked breasts. Dumarest gripped it, tore it from her shoulders, moved tensely to where the Monitor stood.

"Your name," he said again. "What was your name? Were you a man? A woman? Did you know love and hate? Can you remember what it was to feel? The touch of wind on your cheeks, the pressure of lips given in a kiss? Who were you?"

"You will return to your bench and wait. You will obey. You will—"

Dumarest threw the jacket.

It flew high, swirling, falling between the uplifted hands to settle on the painted mask, the glowing eyes. As it left his hand Dumarest threw himself towards the Monitor, blinded now beneath the muffling garment. His left hand hit the floor, the arm serving as a pivot around which swept his body; the full weight of his mass directed at the knee of the Monitor, his boot slamming into the joint.

Metal yielded, plates driven inward to ruin the inner mechanism, the limb distorted into a crooked angle. As the thing tore the muffling fabric from its lenses Dumarest rolled, sprang to his feet and, stooping, gripped the ankle of the damaged leg. Straightening he pulled upwards and outwards, twisting; using the limb as a lever to overthrow the heavy mass. As the Monitor crashed to the floor, he turned and ran.

He was barely in time. As he ran past a connecting passage he saw the bulk of Monitors striding towards him, aid summoned by the one he had felled. An opening stood to his right; he dived through it, crossed the compartment beyond and headed for another passage. It opened on a wide chamber filled with benches, the shadowless glow bright with the searing beams of lastorches. Monitors, lenses masked, stooped over mechanisms lying on the benches; metal plates, limbs, the various parts of others of their kind looking like the fragments of discarded, ancient armour.

An assembly belt over which they worked, apparently heedless of the figure which moved cautiously along the wall.

A pile of fabricated metal lay on a low trolley. Dumarest reached it, crouched behind it, eyes searching the area for a weapon. Against metal his knife was useless, but the torches made a good substitute. He inched forward to where one lay on the edge of a bench and with a sudden rush touched it, snatching it up and racing to where a continuous belt rose from an opening in the floor. A conveyor fitted with platforms on which a man, or Monitor, could stand. It rose to turn at a point ten feet above the floor, descending to a lower level. Dumarest sprang to a platform and, as it carried him down a featureless shaft, examined the torch he had stolen.

It was unfamiliar, but bore certain characteristics; the inbuilt power source which made it portable, the controls which activated and focused the beam. He adjusted it to minimum diameter and maximum length, obtaining a shaft of searing destruction a foot long which would slice through the toughest alloys as if they had been butter.

On the next level, a Monitor was waiting.

Dumarest gave it no time to speak or act, jumping from the platform before it had dropped level with the floor; the beam of the torch became a lance which blasted the eyes, the painted face, falling to shear through a reaching arm, a supporting ankle. As the thing fell he was running again, face dewed with sweat despite the chill of the air, heart pounding in the desperate need for haste.

Already the Monitors must be alerted. The passages filled with the things, as they closed in on where he would be found; moving into position on the basis of some mathematically precise pattern. The one fact which gave him a chance.

Machines were not men. Even with their residual brains, the Monitors would be directed by Camolsaer and a machine would work on the basis of strict logic. In order to survive Dumarest had to outguess it; use his intuition and natural speed to dodge, to gain time.

To destroy, to distract, to disorganize.

A panel opened to reveal massed wires which he cut with a single stroke of the torch. Wires which could and would be repaired, but which now were useless to carry information from the watching, electronic eyes. A heavy door slammed behind him, which he welded fast in the face of advancing Monitors. More wires. A heavy conduit which flared with released energy; molten droplets spattering his tunic, burning his face, his hair. A cleated ramp down which he ran, to halt before a blank wall.

Behind him came the pad of advancing feet.

Dumarest turned, eyes searching the place where he

stood. A dead end; but that in itself was illogical. No human would construct such a place and, if not a human, then certainly not a machine. Therefore, the wall could not be blank. It had to be a door, now sealed; a protective device for what lay beyond.

Metal flared as he applied the torch, droplets oozing, dripping like thick treacle, the beam bursting through into the space beyond. Dumarest moved it in a tight circle, carefully, resisting the impulse to hurry, to waste effort and power. Behind him the sound of advancing feet grew louder; the Monitors must be at the head of the ramp, already coming towards him.

"Man Dumarest. You will cease what you are doing. You will obey."

The ends of the circle had almost joined, a bare portion remaining, as Dumarest felt the touch of a metal hand, the grip of the fingers on his shoulder. He spun, snarling; the beam of the torch slashing at the torso, steadying to burn into the metal, through it, into the controlling brain beneath.

From the grill came a vibrant drone, a mechanical scream; and the hand at his shoulder closed, tightening, pulping the flesh, grinding against the bone. Dumarest swung up the torch, severing the hand, throwing his weight against the dead Monitor. As it fell to block the advance of another Monitor he turned, lifting his foot and slamming his heel against the disk of metal he had cut from the door. The remaining portion snapped with a metallic ringing. Throwing the torch before him he dived headfirst through the opening, plastic smoking as he touched the red hot edges, pain searing his legs, his arms.

Beyond lay a short passage, another door which was descending from a slot above. Dumarest snatched up the torch and threw himself at the narrowing gap; hitting the floor, sliding, feeling weight hit his legs as he jerked them clear. A blast of the torch and the panel was welded fast.

Turning, he looked at Camolsaer.

It stood in the center of a vast chamber, a smoothly rising mass of dull metal ringed with terminals; a main console which bore glowing lenses, a chair fashioned of dark metal set before it as if for some high dignitary.

Around it, flanking the walls, broken only by the spaces of closed doors and arched openings, stood a mass of small screens, each alive with glowing color. Monitors to check the upper installations, the terminals of the eyes which kept constant watch.

Dumarest saw some of them limned with flame, others dark with roiling smoke; Monitors busy with extinguishers, men and women running in panic, an enclosure in which children huddled, safely protected by watchful guardians.

Screens which had been installed when? Watched by whom? Certainly not Camolsaer; the machine would have direct input, and no fabrication would have considered it necessary to construct a chair fashioned for a human shape.

And the thing at which he looked, the smoothly rising metal, the perfectly machined visible parts, could not be the whole construct. That would be far below, carefully designed, served by mechanisms for maintenance and control.

Dumarest walked towards it, carefully studying the floor. It was smooth, set with a tesselated design of red and black, polished to a dull sheen. A ring of benches stood ten feet from the wall, broken into equal segments. Beyond them, barely visible, set behind the chair, showed the outlines of a trap door. A means of access to the regions below. Natural enough if men had built this place; technicians would have to be allowed admission to the regions which held the bulk of the machine.

Dumarest stood on it, moving his feet from edge to edge, feeling the surface yield a little. He pressed harder and the spot beneath his boot sank; the far end of the trap rising to reveal a narrow stair, a dimly lit opening from which came a gust of frigid air.

Ten feet down the stair widened into a platform; more stairs continuing the descent. To the side nearest the chair stood the humped bulk of a complex lattice, from which came a numbing chill. Other machinery could be seen further down; electronic apparatus of unfamiliar pattern, snaking conduits supported on rigid frames.

There would be more lattices lower down, crystals set in containers of liquid helium; the memory banks and directive apparatus of the gigantic whole.

Dumarest placed one foot on the head of the stair then paused, shivering.

Men had built this place. The Cyclan perhaps, a nagging doubt; but if men had made it, then it could be used. And there were things he needed to know.

Sitting in the chair, he rested the flat of his palm on the plate inset into one of the arms.

"Dumarest. Who built you?"

A fraction of a pause and then a cold, flat, emotionless voice.

"The Larchi. A band of men who held the belief that technology could solve all human problems."

"Not the Cyclan?"

"An unfamiliar term."

"Search your banks. Find relative associations." Dumarest described a cyber in detail, the organization to which he belonged. "Could they be the Larchi?"

"No."

Dumarest relaxed a little, yet he had to be sure.

"Are you in contact with anyone on or off this planet?"

"No."

"Is anyone in contact with you?"

"No."

A pounding came from the door by which he had entered. Turning, he saw the panel bulge from the impact of heavy blows. The Monitors, frustrated for a while by the welds, but they wouldn't be frustrated for long.

He said, quickly, "Withdraw all Monitors from the immediate vicinity."

"That directive cannot be obeyed."

"Tell them to cease all activity."

A moment, and then the pounding stopped. At least he had gained a little time. Glancing again at the screens, he saw that more now showed fire and smoke. Arbush and the others were doing a good job.

"The upper installations of the city are in danger. Send all available help to confine the destruction."

"Sufficient help has been provided."

"Send more."

"Sufficient has been provided."

It was like arguing with an echo. Dumarest looked at the door, sensing the Monitors beyond, the others who would be waiting. If he was to escape there was little time and yet, he felt there was more he could do. A trick, perhaps? He remembered something a computer man had once told him. Machines are idiots; by a simple paradox they can be totally incapacitated. And Camolsaer was no more than a machine.

He said, "The next thing I say to you will be the truth." A pause, then he added. "Everything you have learned or heard is a lie."

If the truth, then the penultimate sentence had to be a lie. But if it was a lie, then the ultimate sentence could not be the truth.

A paradox which would not have occupied the attention of a man for longer than he cared; but for a machine based on the iron rules of logic it presented a problem which had to be solved.

And while the thing was occupied, he would add to the confusion.

Torch in hand he ran down the stairs, slamming the trap shut behind him. Welded, it would stay firm. Breath vaporing from the cold, Dumarest ran down the stairs to the platform, eyes searching for points of greatest potential damage. That conduit, cut, would drop to touch that machine and reduce it to molten ruin. A hole burned in the container would release the coolant and perhaps destroy some of the memory banks. A strut burned free would sag and weaken the balance of a support, which might yield a fraction to ruin the arrangement of a monitoring device.

And, above all, he had to find a way out.

The noise was nothing he had ever heard before; the panic totally outside his experience. Adara stood, dazed, frightened at what they had done, the chaos all around.

"Here!" Eloise thrust a bundle of burning rag into his hands. "Set some more fires. Hurry!"

She was a woman possessed, hair bound with a strip of golden braid, her face smudged with soot and ashes. In the daubed mask her eyes burned with a savage intensity, a horrible gloating which he had never seen before. A woman taking her revenge on the place which had held her for so long.

The city which had saved her life.

But she was beyond thinking of that. Remembering all the good things of the past. The wine and talk and loving which had come to fill his days. Now all that was over, as was the calm routine he had known; the smooth tide of life broken only by the Knelling. And, without her, he would have accepted even that. Met it with tranquility, accepting conversion as the due price to be paid for a lifetime of cossetted ease.

"Hurry, you fool!" She screamed at him as he stood, the burning rag in his hands, a distant expression on his face. "More fires! Burn every room you can reach! Send this damned prison to ashes!"

A wish which she knew would never be realized. The fires were too small for that, more smoke than flame; the fabrics smouldering, treated fibers resisting the heat. And the fire she had started with bared wires and a scrap of cloth hadn't done what she'd hoped. The Monitors had been too quick, too fast with their extinguishers. If it hadn't been for the panic, they wouldn't have stood a chance.

That had saved them. Men and women, terrified, running without aim or purpose, thinking only to escape the unknown. The people had blocked the Monitors, provided cover under which they had worked, setting fire after fire; moving from room to room, spreading smoke and flame even into the assembly rooms, some of the work areas.

"Eloise!" Arbush came bustling towards her. A man blocked his path and he slammed him aside with the heel of his hand. "More distraction to the south. The Monitors are still guarding the store."

"You're sure?"

"I've seen them." The minstrel glared at Adara. "What's the matter with him? Doped?"

"Dazed. We're destroying his world." Eloise snatched the rag from his hands before he could be burned. Deliberately, she slapped his face. "Adara! Listen to me. You work with us or we'll leave you behind. You understand? We'll leave you to the Knelling. Now get some more rag and set some more fires."

A room stood to his left, the door open, the chamber deserted. From the bed he stripped the covers, wadded them into a rough cylinder, and ignited the end from the smouldering embers she had knocked to the floor. Back in the room he fired the bed, the curtains; retreating from the wisps of flame, the rising smoke. In the corridor, a Monitor was waiting.

"Man Adara. You will drop what you are holding."

A padded foot trod out the flames.

"Man Adara, explain."

"I saw fire," he babbled. "I thought—that is I tried—I mean—" He broke off, helpless to lie, to break the conditioning of a lifetime. Numbly he waited for the Monitor to seize him, to carry him to a deserved punishment.

"Run!" Flame rose before the painted mask, the glowing lenses. Arbush had thrown burning fabric over the head. "Run, you fool!"

Run to where? The Monitor had known him, how could there be escape? He felt a hand clamp his wrist; a face, eyes slitted, teeth bared thrust close to his own.

"Listen," snapped Arbush. "We're fighting for our lives, understand? You've already done enough to be torn apart on some worlds I could name. No matter what you do now, it can't be worse. And remember Earl. He's relying on us. Now, damn you, get to work before I break your stupid neck!"

A hard man, as Eloise was a hard woman. Animals the both of them, but neither as hard as Dumarest. In the societies from which they came, how could he hope to survive? Adara felt the constriction of his stomach; the familiar, pre-Knelling trepidation, and forcibly squared his shoulders. The minstrel was right. He was committed. Now he had no choice but to continue.

And, oddly, it became easy.

It was almost a game; the defiance of the Monitors, the spreading of the fire. He felt a strange superiority over the others who ran, screamed and stood waiting for guidance. They didn't know what was happening; to them their safe, ordered world had fallen apart.

The tools!" Arbush was at his side. "Don't forget the tools."

"The fires?"

"Eloise can continue with those. She's enjoying it." The minstrel grinned. "Feeling better now? I thought so. There's a relief in knowing you've taken the final step and there's no going back." His hand reached out, gripped, pulled Adara into a room. "Be silent!"

They waited as a Monitor passed, foam spurting from the extinguisher in its hands.

"Slow," said Arbush. "Earl was right. The Monitors aren't used to anything like this and don't know how to handle it."

"Would you?"

"Sure. I'd open the windows and dump the burning

fabrics outside. The walls are of stone and can't be burned. The wind would clear the smoke and once that's gone the people would regain their calm. They shouldn't be here, anyway. If those Monitors had sense, they'd have herded them into one of the large rooms long ago. Now, let's get those tools."

They were hidden under the coverlet in Adara's room, where they had taken them before starting the fires. Two hammers, a pointed bar flat at one end, a wrench used for loosening the caps of small containers of pigment. Arbush pursed his lips as he examined them.

"The bar's too short, we won't get much leverage; and the hammers are too light. The wrench is useless." He hefted it in his hand. "Damn it. Was there nothing else?"

"You were with me," reminded Adara. "You saw what there was."

"Maybe we tried the wrong place. Is there any room fitted out to do heavy repairs?"

"No. All that's done below."

"Acid?" Arbush shook his head. "No. Too dangerous. Camolsaer would never supply it. What then? What the hell can we use?" He beat his hands together in agonized frustration. "Damn it! I wish Earl was here!"

Chapter Thirteen

He was in a shaft three feet square, inching upwards with painful deliberation. Below him lay the bulk of Camolsaer, apparatus turned into cooling slag; containers ruptured, crystals shattered, severed cables still alive with sparkling energy. A conduit had led him to the foot of the shaft, a ventilator which narrowed as he climbed; blocked with grills which he had burned away while the lastorch held power, discarding it to use his knife when it had failed.

Now, supported only by the traction of his boots and hands, he climbed up to where a patch of light shone in the darkness.

Noise came through it; shouts, screams, the scent of burning, wisps of acrid smoke which caught at his lungs. Higher and he saw the grill, crossed bars set in a sturdy frame. He locked his fingers between them, moved his feet up behind him opposite to the grill, his body bent, cramped in the narrow space. He turned, the nape of his neck against the bars, the upper reaches of his shoulders and, with the full strength of his body, thrust his legs against the far wall.

For a moment the grill resisted and then, with a tearing of metal, it yielded; allowing his head and shoulders to pass through, hands to free themselves to grip the edges of the opening before the weight of his legs and hips could pull him back down the shaft.

A jerk and he was falling to the floor of a corridor, ten feet below.

A woman screamed at the sight of him, turning to bump into a man, the pair of them running down the passage in sudden panic. To one side a body lay in a pool of blood; the head crushed, splinters of glass from a shat-

tered bottle lying in a carmine pool. The victim of someone who hoped to escape the Knelling, lying ignored, the
desired constituents of his body going to waste. A sure
sign of the disorganization of the Monitors, the disruption
he had caused.

The pair had run from where smoke billowed at the
mouth of a chamber. Dumarest headed towards it, saw a
Monitor standing helplessly before a fuming mass of vegetation, caught a glimpse of a wild figure setting more
tanks aflame.

"Eloise!"

"Earl!" She came running towards him, almost unrecog-
nizable; her gown torn, face, arms and hands dark with
soot, hair frizzled from too-near flame. "Earl! Thank God
you made it!" Her arms wrapped around him, tight, demanding; the pressure of her body equalling that of her
lips.

"Eloise!" With an effort he pushed her away. "Where
are the others?"

"In Adara's room, I guess." She stared at him, her eyes
wide. "My God, you look a mess. Your clothes! Your
face!" Her hand lifted to touch the spots of burn, the
seared patches of skin. "Earl?"

"I'm all right." He coughed as smoke caught at his
lungs. "Did they get the flying units?"

"I don't know. I've been busy." She gestured at the
havoc she had caused. "I guess we've won. The Monitors
don't seem to care."

For now, but not for long. They were self-motivated
units capable of independent decisions; disorganized now
only because of the lack of direct orders from Camolsaer.
And even that wouldn't last. Already repair units must be
at work on the machine.

"Look at them, Earl. Those damned machines don't
know which way to turn. And look at the fires. I started
them. I did it. This is the finest day of my life."

"It'll be the last, if you don't hurry."

"Fire," she said dreamily. "The poor man's friend. I
heard someone say that once and didn't know what he
was talking about. I know now. It's something I'll remember. Just a spark and everyone's equal. More than equal.
A poor man has nothing to lose, nothing to go up in
flames."

She was transported, almost in ecstasy, something cruel

and primitive in her nature responding to the destruction. Coldly Dumarest slapped her cheek, streaks appearing on the sooted flesh.

"Earl! You—"

"You're forgetting what this is all about." He gestured at the flames. "We've no time to waste while you gloat. We need food, clothes; a lot of things."

"Clothes?"

"You think you can travel like that?" He looked at her torn gown, the naked flesh it revealed. "The cold would kill you within minutes. And you could use a bath."

"Earl?"

"A cold bath," he snapped. "Maybe it will shock some sanity into you. Now let's get moving."

On the way he stopped at a terminal, resting his hand on the plate.

"Dumarest. What is the external weather?"

"Cold. Some wind. Snow expected."

"How soon?"

"Before dark."

"Direction of wind?"

"From the south."

Bad news; worse was the fact that Camolsaer still seemed to be functioning. At least it was answering questions in a precise manner. Dumarest tested it further.

"There is a dead man close to this terminal."

"Dead . . . dead . . . dead . . ."

"Fires are spreading. Compartment 34 is flooded. A Monitor has been crushed in room 812."

A buzz came from the grill—the section of the mechanical brain dealing with variable factors was obviously inoperative.

Dumarest said, "Where is Dras?"

Again the buzz. Satisfied, he turned from the installation.

"What was that all about?" Eloise was puzzled. "I can understand you wanting to know about the weather, but why all the rest?"

"A test. The weather report must be on a different circuit. The main thing is that Camolsaer no longer knows what is going on in the city."

"You wrecked it, Earl."

"Not wrecked, it was too big for that; but I managed to

damage it a little. Let's hope the damage will last long enough."

"Long enough?"

"For us to leave the city."

Arbush had been busy. He was surrounded by a mass of clothing; soft furs, garments of warm fabric, boots, hats, an assortment which Adara had gathered from a dozen rooms. Now the man stood at the ledge before the serving hatch.

"Eloise!" He turned as she entered the room, his face brightening, some of the shadows lifting from his eyes. "My dear, I thought you were hurt. I wanted to look for you but—"

"I wouldn't let him," interrupted Arbush. "Not until we had everything ready. It's good to see you, Earl. Success?"

"Of a kind." Dumarest looked at the clothes, then pushed the woman towards the bathroom. "Strip and get washed. Dirt is a poor insulator against the cold."

"You'll join me, Earl?"

He ignored the invitation, turning to stare at the minstrel where he sat, his face hard.

"Why didn't you get the units?"

"We tried, Earl. Three times. Once we managed to get a wedge started against the lock, but a Monitor arrived and brushed us away. I tried to distract it with fire, but it was no good. The damned thing was still there when we left." Arbush shrugged, glancing at Adara. "So I thought it best to do what we could."

"I failed," said Adara. "I did my best, but it wasn't good enough. Arbush is being kind."

"What are you doing?"

"Ordering food." The minstrel waved to where bundles stood close to the door. "Meats, pastes, oils, food and things to provide fuel. Some wine; they didn't have brandy."

"The means to start a fire?"

Arbush lifted a can tied to a thong, smoke oozing from ragged holes punched in the metal.

"Burning rag," he explained. "Give it a swing and it will flare to life. A thing I learned on Falfard."

As Dumarest had learned it long ago; a primitive method of transporting fire, simple, cheap, effective.

"We'd better carry one each," he said. "And ropes? Did you make some rope?"

Arbush had been thorough. Strips of fabric had been plaited into tough cords, the cords again plaited to form lengths of rope. Dumarest tested one, frowning. They were too short to give real aid if they had to climb, but they would serve to join one to the other. An essential piece of equipment in case of emergency. And a length of rope had many uses.

Adara said, wonderingly, "Earl, all these preparations. I thought we were going to fly over the ice, not walk."

"We may have to do both."

"But the units—"

"We haven't got them yet." Dumarest softened his tone a little; the man couldn't help being what he was. "We've travelled over the ice, you haven't. The units could fail, anything; and only a fool doesn't plan for an emergency. Eloise!"

"Coming, Earl!"

She was naked, unabashed, her skin dusted with powder, fresh paint on her lips and nails; the upper lids of her eyes thick with a blue shadow flecked with silver. More silver bound her hair.

Arbush sucked in his breath. "My lady, you are beautiful!"

She smiled at the compliment, her eyes on Dumarest.

"You wanted me, darling?"

"Get dressed." He was curt, seeing the look in Adara's eyes, knowing the danger of a man who could have lost the wish and will to live. "Adara, help her. Plenty of layers, topped with the thickest furs you can find. Never mind about appearance. Just cover her up so as to keep her warm. Yourself also. We must all get ready."

When finished they looked grotesque; shapes padded and tied almost beyond recognition, faces narrowed beneath enclosing hoods.

Sweating, Arbush distributed the bundles; tying his own, with the neck of the gilyre protruding, to his belt. They were ready to go, but one thing remained to be done.

"Adara, listen to me." Dumarest faced the man, holding his eyes. "There's one thing you've got to remember. You can't lose. Always bear that in mind. If you haven't realized it yet, you're as good as dead. No matter what you do now you can't make things worse. Do you understand?"

"Yes, Earl. Arbush has already explained all that."

"I'm not asking if you know it. I want to know if you accept it. In here." Dumarest rested a finger over the man's heart. "In your guts. You've got to want to survive."

The instinct which in him was so strong, in others so unaccountably weak. He had seen it on a dozen worlds; men sentenced to execution, waiting patiently while watched by a handful of guards. They could have attacked, snatched weapons, died doing it, perhaps; but at least they would have tried. And they would have lost nothing.

"Adara?"

"Yes, Earl. I understand."

Dumarest wasn't so sure. The eyes were still dull, the face lax, resigned. A man moving because of external influences, not because of internal decision. A weakness which could cost them all their lives.

And then, seeing the shift of his eyes as the woman moved, Dumarest knew both the reason and the answer.

"You love her," he said quietly. "You cannot imagine life without her. And you think you have lost her. You haven't. Once we reach safety, she will be yours. I promise that I will not take her with me. She will be yours."

A lie, perhaps; no one could demand that another subjugate personal desires, but at least a part of it was the truth. He repeated it, watching Adara's eyes.

"I shall not take her with me. If you live, you will have all you think necessary for happiness."

Adara brightened, a man in love eager to hear reassurance. "You promise, Earl? You will not take her from me?"

"I promise."

It had to be enough, there was no time for more; already they had lingered too long.

The air at the north gate was clear; the area deserted, aside from a Monitor which stood close to the store which was their target. Too close to suit Dumarest's plan. He walked towards it, hands behind him, the hammers gripped in his fingers, halting well beyond reach of the arms.

"Move!" he snapped. "You're wanted on the upper levels."

"Man Dumarest, you will leave this place." The head turned, glowing lenses registering the presence of the others. "None of you should be here. You will leave immediately.

"No." Dumarest edged forward, moving sidewise, occupying the thing's attention. "You will obey. Go at once to the upper level."

Behind the Monitor he caught sight of movement. Arbush creeping close, one end of the length of rope in his hands; the other held by Adara, the strand taut between them. The Monitor had turned, but was still too close to the store, the locked door they had to force open. Barely three feet of space between its shoulder and the wall—it had to be enough.

"Now!"

Eloise screamed; a high, nerve-stopping sound, shocking in its raw implication of agony. The Monitor glanced towards her, taking one step in her direction and, as the gap widened, Arbush moved.

He lunged like a furred ball, the rope in his hands; thrusting his bulk between the Monitor and the wall, past the tall, metallic figure. As the rope tightened Dumarest sprang, taking three steps forward; lifting his feet as he flung himself at the Monitor, his boots slamming with the full weight of his body against the upper torso. Thrown back by the impact the thing hit the rope, blow and drag working in opposite directions, levers which sent it off-balance to crash to the ground.

Then Dumarest was on it, hammers lifting, falling; smashing the lenses, the elbows, the joints of the legs.

"Quick!" Eloise was at the door, a wedge rammed into the point above the lock. "Hurry, Earl!"

He was already at work, the hammer a blur as he slammed it down, a tool too light for the job; its lack of mass having to be compensated by the muscles of his arms, back and shoulders. Above the sound of the blows, he heard the minstrel's snarl.

"Another of the damned things. Remember, Adara; hold the rope tight, catch its legs and pull."

A plan hastily improvised, depending on shrewd teamwork, the will to survive.

A crash and another Monitor was down; Arbush yelling

as he wielded the other hammer, aiming for the electronic eyes.

"Earl?"

"The bar." He threw the hammer into her hands and snatched the strip of metal. The flattened end slipped into the gap he had made with the wedge, now knocked free. Gripping the far end, he heaved.

"Arbush!" The bar was too short, his strength insufficient. "To me! Eloise, take the rope and work with Adara. Move!"

Dumarest sucked in his breath as the minstrel joined him, plump hands locking over his own.

"On the word. Get ready. Now!"

Again he heaved, legs straddled, back arched, blood darkening his fingernails. Arbush added his strength, pushing, breath rasping, boots clamped against the floor. The bar yielded a little.

"Earl!"

Eloise, her voice high, rising above the drone of an approaching Monitor; but there was no time to look.

"Damn it!" gasped Arbush. "So near—"

He lunged forward as something broke with a rip of metal; his weight hit Dumarest, sending him staggering back, the bar still in his hand. Beyond the rounded figure he could see the woman and Adara, the rope between them looped around the legs of a Monitor; another was advancing, hands extended.

The bar left his hand, hurtling across the fifty feet of space between them to slam its length against the painted face, the glowing eyes.

"The units!" The door of the store was open wide, Arbush delving inside where compact mechanisms hung on brackets; smoothly rounded and shaped metal fitted with an elaborate harness. "We've got them—but there's no time."

Dumarest thrust him aside. In a row, held in clips, stood a line of squat cylinders fitted with grips, a movable projection. He snatched one, saw the orifice at one end, the sights on the barrel and found the release. A weapon which, of necessity, would be rendered harmless before being stored. Unloaded, perhaps, certainly uncocked. He dragged at the projection, felt it slide, heard a soft click.

"Down!" he shouted. "All of you, down!"

He hit the floor as they obeyed, cradling the weapon,

aiming it at the Monitor who had fallen and was now regaining its feet; closing his finger on the trigger as the
sights came into line. A thread of fire spat from the muzzle reaching towards the torso, to dissolve in a gush of
flame, a roaring explosion.

A second shot and the other Monitor joined the first,
lying in broken wreckage; shattered plates blasted open to
reveal inner mechanisms, the freed liquids of a crystal
container, the pulped mass of the residual brain.

"God!" Eloise rose, hands clamped to her ears, a thread
of blood showing at one nostril. "That was close, Earl.
You damned near burst my eardrums."

"You'll live. Get into one of the units."

"What?" She had forgotten the hands at her ears. Dropping them, she came towards him. Irritably Dumarest gestured her aside.

"Don't stand in the line of fire. It won't take long for
more Monitors to get here. Now get into one of those
flying units. Adara! You know how they are used. Instruct
us."

Basically they were simple; a power-pack activating
anti-gravity plates, straps which went over the shoulders,
around the torso, up between the thighs. The lift was from
the base of the pack, controlled by a simple switch. Direction was governed by movements of the body.

"First you lift," said Adara. "When you get high
enough, you throw your head and upper body forward.
There are automatic compensating plates so that you don't
fall. If you can manage to remain straight, with your head
in the direction you want to go, you'll get maximum velocity."

"And if you want to twist, face back in the direction
from which you came?"

"You can do it, Earl. You'll have to adjust the lift, of
course; otherwise you'll keep rising." Adara made a helpless gesture. "Mostly it's a matter of practice."

Which the Monitors had and they did not. And there
was no time to do more than test, to see if the units held
power.

Already the Monitors were arriving, tall shapes glinting
as they strode down the corridors leading to the gate.
From the store Dumarest handed each one a gun, tucking
another beneath his harness. Adara looked blankly at the
one in his hands.

"What do I do with it, Earl?"

"You cock it, so. Then you point it at what you want to hit and squeeze that trigger. Now outside, all of you!"

The last to go, he paused at the door; turning, the weapon levelled in his hands. The Monitors were close; fragments whined, striking the wall to one side, smoke and flame tainting the air as he blasted them to ruin. Again he fired, sending missiles into the open store, filling it with destruction; explosions occurred as the contents erupted in a burst of energy which sent metal running in a molten tide.

The other units ruined, the weapons; time gained as they got away.

Outside the cold struck like a knife, numbing exposed cheeks, hands and fingers. Dumarest donned thick gloves and hit the control, rising with the others, passing them, slowing as he made an adjustment.

"Arbush, stay close!"

The minstrel was high and drifting to one side. With a jerk he twisted in mid-air, legs lifting as he levelled out in an upward-sloping glide. Eloise, with her dancer's agility, had quickly mastered the elementary system of control. She reached for the plump shape, caught at a strap and brought him into line. Adara was far to the south.

"Catch him!" Dumarest caught up with the others and gripped the woman's arm, nodding towards Adara. "Keep up with him. Hold his hand, but don't let him get away. We have to stay together."

She twisted, smiling.

"Let him go, Earl. We don't need him."

"He needs us."

"I didn't mean forget him. We just don't need what he can teach us. These things are easy to handle."

For her, perhaps, but not for the minstrel. He darted from side to side; over-compensating, dipping to rise, to twist. Dumarest passed over him, gripped his other arm.

"We'll hold him between us, Eloise. Now let's get Adara."

He had slowed and was waiting. Together, like a flock of ungainly birds, hands clasped for mutual aid, they rose up and flew away from the city.

Eloise laughed as she saw it shrink, to dwindle and lose itself in the wilderness.

"The end, Earl. Five years of hell and now I'm free. Free. And I owe it all to you."

"We're not clear yet, Eloise."

"We will be," she said confidently. "And when we are, I'll show you what gratitude really means. What a woman in love can do for her man. When we're alone I'll—"

A gust of wind drowned the rest of her words and Dumarest was glad of it. Adara would be listening, but more important was the woman's attitude of mind. While she dreamed of the future, she would tend to ignore the dangers of the present.

Releasing his grip Dumarest turned and looked towards the rear, seeing nothing. As he resumed his former position Arbush muttered, "Earl, it's damned cold."

It was freezing. The wind was against them, a frigid blast which robbed their bodies of heat. Flying took little physical effort and they were inviting hypothermia, despite the muffling garments.

"We'll land after a while," said Dumarest. "Walk on for a time and warm ourselves up."

"When?"

"Soon." It would have to be soon. Adara was hunched, trembling; Eloise now silent, her face a deathly white. Softened by the city, they were ill-suited to rigour. "In an hour."

An hour of flight; then twenty minutes in which they stumbled over the ice, beating numbed hands, generating heat by the activity of their bodies; then into the air again always into the wind, always heading towards the south.

And, at dusk, came the snow.

Chapter Fourteen

Arbush chuckled, rubbing his hands over the smoking glow of burning rag smeared with oil, the light dancing on his face, the thrown-back hood.

"Remember the last time we camped like this, Earl? Hurt, you nearly dead, down to the last drop of brandy? We found a cave then and had a candle of sorts. Now we've got luxury."

Eloise said, "You must be joking."

"No, I mean it. A dry cave, no wind to speak of, food, a fire, some wine, good clothes; what else do you need?"

"A song."

"Sleep. We've had a hard day." Dumarest glanced to where Adara lay slumped on the floor. He was breathing deeply, his eyelids jerking as if he dreamed. Lifting his boot Dumarest poised the heel over the fire, then changed his mind. The glow was small, the mouth of the cave blocked with the units and packs; the light would not show outside. And it would be a convenience if they had to move fast, a comfort for anyone if they woke.

Eloise, perhaps. Adara. The man had remained silent as they ate, nursing his food, his wine; a man lost in the maze of unpleasant thoughts. Brooding over what he had heard, or anticipating what was to come, the new life he would have to lead. Well, he would learn to survive or he would succumb.

And there were other things to worry about. The flying units—Dumarest had no idea how long they would last. With the wind against them, they had made small progress and the units could fail. A fact which he had recognized, but had been forced to accept. As he had been forced to lose the opportunity of questioning Camolsaer, which he would have liked.

To ask if it had known the whereabouts of Earth.

It could, possibly, have known. Those who had built it long ago might have fed the knowledge to its banks. A few more minutes and the answer could have been his. But those few minutes might have cost him his life. Monitors had been in the lower region. Special units which had ignored the imposed directive, if the directive had been imposed at all. Machine or not, Camolsaer would have obeyed the dictates of survival.

He jerked, suddenly aware that he had dozed; aware too of something beside him, of the warm pressure of lips on his cheek.

"Earl! Earl, my darling! Earl!"

Eloise, awake, her breath warm. A whisper which he matched.

"What do you want?"

"You, my darling. You. Earl, how long must I wait?"

Her cheeks were flushed, the skin febrile, the eyes liquid with passion.

"Earl, I love you. You know that."

"So?"

"I need you." She saw the glance of his eyes and thrust her face before his own. "The others? What the hell does it matter? Anyway they are asleep. Even if they weren't, I wouldn't care."

"Maybe not," he said gently. "But I would."

"Why? Are you ashamed? No, you've never been ashamed of anything. Shy then? No, not that. Then what, Earl? Don't you want me?"

"What I want isn't too important. Not just now. The thing is we're a group and we have to help each other to survive. This is no way to do it."

"Because of Adara? Are you afraid of him, Earl?"

"And if I said that I was?"

"You'd be lying." Her voice strengthened a little. "You're not afraid of anything that walks or talks or lives, on any world anywhere. You don't know the meaning of fear. You can't. You're that kind of a man."

"If you think that then you're a fool," he said harshly. "You're not talking about bravery, but stupidity. There are a lot of things I'm afraid of. One of them is flying close to a man with a grudge against me and a deranged mind. A man with a gun, which he might decide to use at any moment without warning."

"Then take it from him."

"And demean his pride?" He added, as she made no answer. "A man doesn't need a gun to kill, Eloise. And his target needn't be myself."

"You're thinking of me," she said quickly. "That means you care for me. Then why not leave him, Earl? Get rid of the danger? Kill him if you have to. You could do it."

"Yes," he admitted. "I could do it if I had to. And if he was hurt, dying and in pain I would. But tell me, Eloise, just what has he done to you that you want to see him dead?"

"Done? Why nothing, Earl. He—"

"Saved your life." Dumarest glanced to where he lay. Quietly he added, "When you think about it, Eloise, it seems a poor reward."

Adara had been dreaming; a nightmare in which he ran from something terrible, straining every muscle and yet making no progress. And faces had watched him as he ran, laughing faces which had turned and kissed, to face him again with cynical amusement.

Eloise, whom he had lost.

Dumarest, who had won her affection.

He stirred and opened his eyes. The fire was a bare glow in the darkness, an ember which threw a low, ruddy light in which shapes rested, shadows thick around and between. Two of them seemed to be lying close together, too close; and with sudden jealousy he added fuel to the ember, blowing it to life, turning to verify his suspicions.

He had been mistaken. Dumarest was alone; the impression that another lay at his side was a trick of the light. And yet surely there had been the murmur of voices, the rustle of movement? Or had that been, like the smiles and kisses, a part of his dream?

Tiredly he looked around. Arbush was a mound, his face a blur. Eloise was another, her back towards him, a tangle of hair falling over her hood. He looked again at Dumarest; the stranger who had come to ruin his life, the violent man whom the woman had chosen.

Violence, why did she love it so much?

And, if she did, and he should prove to be the more violent of both men, would she again turn to him with love in her eyes?

If he should kill Dumarest?

He felt himself tense at the alien concept and fought the ingrained conditioning of the past. Old habits had been replaced by new, and the man himself had told him that he had nothing to lose. To kill then, to strike and prove himself the master; to take the fruits of victory, the love he had known.

And the man himself had provided the means.

He turned and reached for one of the weapons; lifting it to stare along the barrel at the hard face, hard even in sleep. A simple pressure and it would be done. But he had seen the thing work, the destruction it caused. To fire it in this confined space would be to kill them all.

Carefully he placed it aside and again studied the sleeping man.

The eyes, perhaps; his fingers gouging, blinding, gaining time in which to kill at his leisure. He sweated at the thought of it; how could he ever rob another of his vision? The throat then; his fingers tightening, stopping the breath. Or the gun, not fired, but used as a club. His hand crept towards it.

"Try it," said Arbush quietly, "and you'll be dead before you know it."

"You know?"

"I saw."

"But the gun? I—"

"You hadn't cocked it. If you had, the noise would have woken Earl at once." The minstrel rose from where he lay, hunching as he warmed his hands at the fire. "He looks asleep, and he is, but only as an animal sleeps. One move towards him, a touch, and he will waken ready to kill. I recognize the signs."

"Does he always sleep like that?"

"Not always, he's a man, not a beast; but he's learned to survive. And you worry him. Did you know that the woman wanted to leave you behind?"

"No! She couldn't. She—"

"She's in love with Earl. A woman in love is rarely sane and never to be blamed. A man either. Earl knows that, which is why you are here."

"He promised me that he wouldn't take her." Adara looked from one to the other. "He swore to me that he would leave her."

"And he will. Earl isn't looking for a woman. He is searching for something more important than that."

"Earth, she told me."

"Earth." Arbush sighed. "A dream, perhaps, but one which rules his life. Which gives him the reason for living, perhaps; we should all have a reason for that. Once I thought I had it, but for me the dream didn't last. I had the gift of music and the ability to make a song. Small things some would say; to me they were the gate to adventure, the means to achieve paradise. In a way I found it. For a few weeks it was real. In the city was everything I had ever longed for. I tasted it, revelled in it; now it is gone. But, my friend, such is life."

"Endless disappointment?"

"In a way, as women are. Each offers untold joys and each, somehow, fails to deliver what we expect. And always there are surprises. The plain one who is passed by at a glance can, when passion rules her, dominate the universe of a man's being. The one who is lovely to look at can be as cold as the ice around us. And, after all, what is a woman? Surely she is something which can be shared? Once you had her, now she yearns for another, but have you lost all? Once Earl has gone, what then? She will still remain."

Adara said, slowly, "I wanted to kill him."

"You are not the first."

"I wanted to take his life because of Eloise." Adara shook his head, baffled. Too much had happened too fast. "Tell me, am I mad?"

"You are tired," said the minstrel. "And maybe a little feverish. At such times, thoughts are rarely clear. What you need is some wine." He reached for the bottle which he had warmed against his bulk. "Drink, my friend, and relax. All will be well."

They left at dawn, rising into air which was clear and crisp; the snow which had fallen during the night a soft blanket of whiteness over the rough terrain. The wind had changed, now blowing from the north in a steady stream; a shift to their advantage. As was the practice they had now gained. No longer was it necessary to lock their hands.

An added advantage for Dumarest who often rose high above the others, to turn and search the empty wastes behind; to dive, gaining speed as he caught up.

"You're worried." Eloise glided to his side, one hand

reaching out to grip his arm, a lever to draw her close.
"You keep looking back. Why, Earl?"

"A precaution."

"You think we could be followed?" It was something
she had never considered. "But how, Earl, and why? The
Monitors wouldn't move without orders from Camolsaer
and you wrecked it."

"I damaged it," he corrected. "And it was minor damage, at best."

Destruction easily repaired and the machine could have
rerouted information channels; cut the destroyed mechanisms from its operational circuits.

She said, "I know more about it than you do, Earl. I
lived with it longer. Camolsaer takes no interest in anything beyond the city. We are well beyond it and so it will
ignore us. The Monitors too."

"Perhaps. I hope so."

"But you aren't sure?" She twisted her head and looked
back, seeing nothing but the endless expanse of ice and
snow over which they flew. "You're thinking of it as a
man," she decided. "A living thing wanting revenge, but
we're talking about a machine. At first, maybe, it would
have tried to get us; but not now. We're too far away."

A comfort he couldn't share. To survive, the city had to
remain in isolation; the reason the Monitors hunted any
Krim who came too near. They had made slow progress
yesterday and had rested during the night. Monitors were
not hampered by the limitations of flesh.

"Earl," she said abruptly. "About last night. What you
said. I guess I was wrong."

"About what?"

"You know." She pointed to where Adara flew, a little
to the front. "But I didn't mean what you thought I did. I
was just worried about you, that's all."

"Not him?"

"Not then. I didn't think. But this morning he was acting strange. He kept looking at me and didn't smile and
barely ate. Could he be sick, Earl?"

"Maybe. Go over to him and keep him company. Try
and cheer him up." Dumarest glanced back and down, as
the minstrel called to him. "Don't get too far ahead."

Arbush was in trouble. He writhed in his harness,
sweating as he manipulated his body, plump hands at the
switch.

"The damned thing's failing, Earl. I've got it on full lift, but I can't keep up."

Dumarest looked down. The terrain had levelled, broken ground lying ahead, the blanket of snow thinning; it was broken by ice-capped teeth, bare rock showing like grey scabs. A bad place to land.

"Drop," he ordered. "Get down fast and wait. We'll join you."

"Earl?"

"Down and fast!" If the unit were to suddenly fail, the man would drop like a stone. Dumarest hit the switch and felt the sluggish response. Advancing to the others he wheeled, slashed a hand across his throat and pointed downwards.

Adara was little help.

"I don't know how long the units are supposed to last, Earl," he admitted. "I've never even thought about it. I just assumed they were inexhaustible. Is there anything you can do?"

Dumarest examined the mechanism. The unit was sealed, three small holes set into the inner surface; a recharging point, perhaps. He could discover no way by which to gain access to the power pack inside.

"Arbush is heavy," he said. "He's got more weight than any of us, so would have used up more power. We'll have to equalize. Eloise, switch units."

"Earl?"

"You're the lightest. Do it." He frowned as, reluctantly, she made the exchange. "We must dump some weight. The wine can go. Most of the fuel. Nearly all of the food. The gilyre—"

"No, Earl!" Arbush was defiant. "Not that. I'd starve first."

"How about the guns?" said Eloise. "Do we need all of them?"

"Dump yours," said Dumarest. "And you too, Adara."

"No, I'd rather not." He stood, face bleak but determined. "Logically, Arbush should get rid of his. It will compensate for the gilyre."

And he needed to retain his own, as a symbol of his pride; the outward sign of his equality with Dumarest.

"Let him keep it, Earl," said Eloise, understanding. "How about clothes? Have we come far enough south to shed a few?"

"No." The wind could change again, and without food they would need the protection of the furs. And they hadn't travelled as far as she thought. "Later, maybe, but not yet. Now let's get moving. Keep close and don't ride too high."

"Does it matter?" Arbush shrugged. "A fall from a hundred feet or a thousand, what is the difference?"

"There must be a safety factor. A reserve of lift, once the power dies. If we're too high we could land, yes, but we would be stuck where we hit. Travelling low, we'll have a chance to squeeze a little more from the units, couple them up, maybe." Dumarest adjusted his harness. "Let's get going."

Up into the air again, keeping close, conscious now of the factor of time and distance covered as never before; passing over the flat terrain, the broken ground, rising a little to escape the turbulent air gusting up from ravaged peaks.

A journey without a break; dead weight took power to lift, power which could carry them on their way. Eloise lagged behind a little and Dumarest slowed to maintain the grouping. Arbush forged ahead beating his hands, the gilyre strung from his belt. A gust of wind caught him from one side and he turned, tumbling like a leaf before regaining his equilibrium. Adara fell back and Dumarest turned towards him; seeing the pale face, the burning eyes, the gun held in the gloved hands.

Seeing also the glinting shapes which fell from the sky.

Chapter Fifteen

~~~~~~~~~~~~~~~~~~~~~~~~~~~~~~~~~~~

They came like arrows shaped like armoured men; three of them, diving from where they had ridden high in the air, almost invisible against the sky. Monitors fitted with units more powerful than their own, armed with weapons more destructive. Flame and smoke rose from the ice, leaving wide craters gaping in the roar of explosions.

"Arbush! Eloise! Down! Find a crevasse and hide!"

Unarmed, they were useless. Dumarest twisted, throwing his body back, face turned upwards; the weapon in his hands firing, aimed by instinct. The foremost Monitor burst in a rain of metallic fragments.

"Adara! Quick! Damn you, man! Open fire!"

He was too slow, forgetting to cock the weapon, fumbling as he jerked at the protrusion. Dumarest snarled, firing again; hitting the switch on his harness to fall as death tore the air where he had been. He rose, the unit sluggish as the Monitors swept past and down, to rise again in a sharp curve towards him. He saw their glowing lenses, the guns aimed and steady, the orifices which would spout missiles to take his life. One he could hit, never both; and one wasn't enough.

"Earl!"

Adara was rising, his face taut, the gun awkward in his hands.

"Turn, you fool!" He was facing the wrong way. "Turn!"

The Monitors were beyond him, a little above as they came in for the kill. Another second and they would open fire. Dumarest tensed, jerked to one side, lifted the gun and closed his finger. Flame blossomed as one of the things died, but the other had already fired.

149

E. C. Tubb

Then Adara was before him, a living barrier against which the missiles burned; to explode, to rip apart flesh and bone, to shower the air with a fine spray of smoking blood.

Dumarest dropped, turned as the Monitor passed; he fired at the head, the missiles hitting the torso, the hips, shattered metal falling to join the tattered bundle which once had been a man.

"Thank god!" As he landed, Arbush came running from a crevasse in which he had only seen the blur of movement, the flash of explosions against the sky. "Earl, I thought it had got you. I saw—"

"Adara." Dumarest looked at the woman. "He saved my life at the cost of his own."

"I'm glad, Earl. Glad that it wasn't you."

"I wish it hadn't been anyone," said Arbush. "In a way, I liked the man. Felt a little sorry for him, I suppose. Well, he's dead now, and at peace." He rubbed thoughtfully at his cheek. "At least we're out of danger."

"For the moment." Dumarest searched the sky, tensed as he saw three more flecks in the distance. "Take those units off. Hurry!"

Elosie frowned. "Why, Earl? We shall need them."

"Do as I say." Tearing at the harness, Dumarest stepped from the tangle of straps. "Those Monitors followed us and more are coming. How do you think they found us?"

"A beacon?" The minstrel was shrewd. "Inside the units, Earl?"

"I think so. What else are we carrying which could contain it. They're homing in on a broadcasting unit. Now get rid of them and hurry!"

A deep crevasse swallowed the machines, Dumarest leading the way from the spot; ducking, keeping under cover, out of sight of the Monitors who had grown in the sky. An overhang gave on to a blind grotto, a dead-end facing the crevasse in which they had dumped the units. Rocks lay before it, the gray stone slimed with ice; he crouched behind them, the others lying flat to the rear.

Arbush whispered, "We dumped the food, Earl. If we lose the units—" He broke off, remembering the past; the bleak and savage time before they had reached the city.

"We'll be alive," said Dumarest.

"True, if they're satisfied with finding the units. But if they should look for us, what then?"

"We pray." Eloise's voice held an ironic amusement. It changed as vibrations tore the air, the shock of explosions shaking the stone on which they lay. "Earl!"

"Be quiet!"

"But, Earl—"

"Damn you, woman! Be silent!"

The units, he knew, had been destroyed, their signalling devices stilled; but unless the Monitors were fools an examination would be made. They would have expected to see the fugitives, could still expect to find them, and they must know that they couldn't be far.

They would be drifting above at this moment, flying slow and low, sensors alerted for sonic vibrations; the unmistakable signs of infra-red radiation which would betray the presence of living tissue.

Something scraped at the end of the tunnel leading to the grotto. A fragment of ice fell, a small stone. Slowly Dumarest reached beside him for the gun, lifted it, steadied it on his arm.

The weapon could, in itself, have betrayed them; but it was the only defence against the things they had. And he couldn't be sure how effective it would be; how many missiles it contained. Only one, perhaps, in which case they were dead. But if it held only three, they had a chance.

Again came the scrape of ice and something dropped from above. He heard a soft inhalation as Eloise sucked in her breath, the rustle as Arbush moved, his urgent whisper.

"Get it, Earl! Quickly, for God's sake!"

Dumarest didn't move, staying frozen, blended into the rocks behind which he lay. One Monitor was in sight; where were the other two?

Something hit the overhang as another metallic shape came into view. Two facing him and one above; out of sight and impossible to reach without showing himself. And the things were fast. It would fire before he could turn and aim.

Unless, somehow, its attention could be distracted.

Dumarest rose, aimed, fired all in one quick movement, the missile bursting against the head of the foremost Monitor; slamming it back against its companion. The weapon it held lifted, firing as the fingers clamped in dying reflex, sending a hail of missiles into the air above where he stood.

An explosion wracked the air as Dumarest sprang from cover, turning in mid-air to see the Monitor above falling, limned with flame; he turned again to send the last shot his weapon contained at the remaining Monitor as it climbed to its feet.

As the echoes died Arbush said, dazed, "God, Earl, I never thought a man could move so fast. You were just a blur."

Speed and luck, which had won the calculated gamble. Looking at the wreckage Eloise said, "What now, Earl?"

"We walk."

"Walk?" Her voice was high, incredulous. "Without food or fuel? A thousand miles or more over this ice? Maybe it would be better to end it now."

"We walk," he said again. "And we try to contact the Krim."

The man was small, plump, his face smooth in its rim of fur. His hands were broad, dark with hair on the backs, the nails blunt and filed short. He wore garments of quilted fabric, warmed by the power-packs at his belt. His name was Juskan, a trader.

"You were fortunate," he said. "If you had handled things differently, made a threatening gesture even; well, you wouldn't be here now."

"Luck," said Arbush. "Earl is loaded with it. I read it in his palm." He dipped again into his bowl of stew, swallowing, chewing a fragment of meat. "Luck," he mused. "Sometimes I wonder if, of all the things a man could wish to be given, that is not the most important. Is there more stew?"

"Help yourself." Juskan gestured to the pot which hung on a tripod over the fire. "How about you?"

Dumarest shook his head. "Later, maybe."

"And you?"

Eloise put aside her bowl, shaking her head. Her face was hollowed, thin with privation, her eyes enormous beneath the level brows. A week, she thought, or had it been longer. Days in which they had crossed the rugged ground, staying always on the skyline; burning garments at night to make a clearly visible flame. And then had come the Krim.

They had arrived like ghosts, furred balls with peaked, suspicious faces; talking only in monosyllables, armed with knives and primitive guns.

And now, incredibly, they were safe.

She leaned back in the low chair, looking at the expanse of the underground cavern to which they had been taken; the walls thick with luminous fungus, the roof crusted with mineral deposits. Such places were to be expected, the Krim had to live somewhere; once explained, it all seemed so obvious.

"They're a primitive people," said Juskan. "They live by hunting and farming the fungus. There is coal in certain regions and they do a little mining. They have a legend that, one day, they will all move to a paradise somewhere in the north."

To the city and, one day, they might take it. Dumarest wondered what would happen then. What would become of the people it now contained?

He said, "Aren't you curious as to what it could be like?"

"No." Juskan shrugged. "I've heard so many legends, one way and another. Every tribe has them and none of them are more than wishful thinking. You crashed, you say?"

"Our flyer got caught in a storm."

"It happens. You chose the wrong time; winter is hard. Not that summer is much better, but there's more chance then. In the air, anyway, not on the ground. When it gets a little warmer, animals come out of hibernation and some of them can be trouble." Juskan leaned forward to examine the pot. "If you don't want any more of this stew, I'll hand it over to the women. They have a taste for what's in it."

Spices and soft meat, dehydrated foods which the man had brought with him. Dumarest watched as a lumpish girl carried the pot over to where a huddle of children sat around a mass of glowing fungus.

"You said you were a trader. After furs?"

"Furs, gems, anything that's going; but mostly I'm after doltchel. The only way to get the Krim to work is to stay with them. My partner and I take it in turns. It isn't so bad, really. The caves are snug and I've got a few comforts." He glanced at the woman. "Treat them right and they play along. And they need what we can bring; knives, guns, ammunition, needles, stuff like that."

Eloise said, "Where do they come from?"

"The Krim?" Juskan shrugged. "Maybe they're the survivors of an early settlement. They could even be true natives. I've never bothered about it."

A man devoid of curiosity, or one who had decided that curiosity didn't pay.

Dumarest said, "Can you get us to Breen? We can pay."

"That helps," admitted the trader. "At least it'll get you a ride, but not for a month at least. My partner will be coming on a raft then. If you can compensate me for the lost load and trouble, I'll take you in." He looked at Eloise. "Is that your woman?"

"Yes," she said quickly.

"There's a small cave you can share. The minstrel can stay with me."

Arbush said, shrewdly, "With comforts?"

"Something can be arranged." Juskan glanced at the gilyre. "Are you any good with that thing?"

"I'm an expert."

"Then you'll have no trouble. The Krim like music. How about a tune now?"

The music rose as a woman guided Dumarest to a cave. A thick covering closed the opening; massed fungus giving light to show a table, chairs, a mass of furs piled for sleeping.

Eloise looked at them. "Earl?"

"Yes?"

"Did you mind me telling Juskan that I was your woman?"

"No."

"Then does that mean—" She stepped closer to him, lifting her hands to his shoulders. "Adara is dead now, Earl; we can't hurt him no matter what we do. And I love you. I want you."

He said, flatly, "When we reach Breen, I leave you."

Perhaps; but, woman-like, she was confident of her power. And she had at least a month to make him change his mind. As the thrum of strings rose from behind the curtain she closed her arms around him, holding him tightly, tighter, her lips a demanding flame.

Breen was a slum, a huddle of shacks interspersed with stone buildings, warehouses, limited repair facilities; the usual conglomeration to be found on any primitive world. Eloise crinkled her nose at the odors; acrid, harsh when compared to the natural smells she had grown accustomed to while living with the Krim. Juskan had gone, dropping them at the field and going about his business. As Dumarest was going about his.

She looked at the field, the ships it contained; a small trader plying among local worlds, a vessel from Prel, another from somewhere beyond the Elmirha Dust. He had been fortunate, the port was unusually busy.

"He won't go," she said. "Earl won't leave me."

"You think that?" Arbush was at her side; a small, somehow shrunken figure, his gilyre nursed in his hands. Absently he plucked a string. "You are being unkind to yourself, Eloise. Earl will do as he said."

As he had stated from the first, as he would do despite their time of passion, of hours spent in love. The time when she had used all her skills to bind him to her; yet, she remembered, never once during that time had he wavered, promised more than he could accomplish. An interlude, she thought bleakly. An episode on his journey. An event which was now over—for her own hope of future happiness she had to accept that.

And, if nothing else, she had memories.

"He will leave us," said Arbush. "He will move on." The movement of his hand on the fret made the note he plucked rise to the thin wail of an empty cry. "Do you think you are alone in your desire to want him to stay? I was nothing when we met; on the lowest rung of the ladder, one step from the mud of the gutter, bound to a swine by debts I couldn't pay. Chains which Earl broke. He saved my life—do you think I can forget that? Do you think that love must always be from a woman to a man?"

"Love?"

"Something deeper than friendship. The feeling a man has for his son. Not love as you know it, perhaps; but the thing which makes a man stand by his comrade, to kill for him, to die for him." Again the plucked string made its empty cry. "We have much in common, you and I."

The stink of taverns, bad food, poor clothing, the edge of poverty. Tunes played for bread and dances given for the sake of thrown coins. Avid faces and reaching hands,

the demands on her flesh as much as her talent; the life
she had once known and had almost forgotten. The stench
had brought it back. The dirt of the settlement, the
remembered faces, the need for money—always the need
for money.

Five years in the city had made her soft.

She said, bleakly, "There was a world I knew once; a
small place with farms and animals and happy children. A
dull place, I once thought, a world without excitement. I
used to watch the ships land and long to ride with them.
And then, one day, I did."

"An old tale," said Arbush. "I could tell one much the
same."

"Would you go back if you could?"

"To the world I left? No. A man has his pride. But
there are other worlds on which a man could settle to end
his days."

"Small worlds," she said. "Places where a man with the
gift of music and the touch of song could make his way.
Teaching, entertaining, making instruments for sale."

"And, where too, a dancer could teach her art," he
pointed out. "As I said, Eloise, we have much in common.
True I am old and have little to offer, but what I have is
yours. Money for passage, enough left over to buy a mod-
est place."

She said, "There's Earl."

He came towards them, touching their hands, the gesture of farewell.

Eloise said, quickly, "You're leaving, Earl. Let us come
with you. To the next world at least."

"No."

"Me, then. Please!"

"To be left among strangers?" Dumarest glanced at the
minstrel. "Here you have a friend."

"Earl!"

"Goodbye, Eloise."

Arbush took her arm as Dumarest walked to where the
ships were waiting, turning her away, leading her towards
the edge of the field.

"It's over," he said gently. "Earl has gone to find his
dream. You can't go with him. No one can. It is something he must do alone."

DAW BOOKS